Pack Triage

By Harlowe Frost

Printed in the United States of America: First Printing, 2023.

ISBN: 978-1-959981-18-3 (eBook)
ISBN: 978-1-959981-17-6 (paperback)

http://www.hannahwillow217.com

Copy/Line Editor: Angela Grimes
Editor: Weslee Imrisek
Formatting: Huckleberry Rahr
Cover Art: Getcovers.com

Coastal Wolves:

1: Pacific Pack

2: Wolf Magic

3: Campus Prowl

4: Loan Wolf

5: Pack Triage

6: Mystical Science

7: Lupine Investigation

Dedication:

We've made it to book five, and I'd really like to thank all of you for reading Coastal Wolves. I write for you and knowing people are enjoying the series warms my heart (and fingers that keep typing more and more!)

I have a group of beta readers and ARC readers who have encouraged me, who I greatly appreciate. Elle Armstrong, Nicole Maness, Shimere Alexander, Betsy Tilton, and many more!

I want to give a special shout out to my editors who slog through all my writing: Weslee Imrisek and Angela Grimes.

Chapter 1 - Starting With a Bang!
Tory

The chaos in the kitchen was as insane as the emergency room. Tory watched as Tamsin and Orin cooked brunch for everyone in the pack house. Tamsin had only been back a month, about a quarter of her reign as alpha, but already things were falling into place. A calm settled over all of them with her return. As calm as anything could be in the craziness of a pack of wolves.

Orin darted by, sliding mugs of his famously fantastic coffee in front of Tory, and Paige, Tamsin's partner. The two of them sat together at the kitchen table, out of reach of danger. *In a pack of wolves who can cook, we need to stay out of trouble!*

Tory sipped her coffee with a sigh. "Orin, did you master coffee because you work from home? You know, The Zesty Bean is only a few blocks away, but man, they have nothing on your coffee."

He chuckled and went back to frying bacon. "Miss my coffee on your early morning shifts?"

She groaned. "You have no idea."

Paige sipped her coffee. "Are you excited about the fireworks? The fourth isn't until Tuesday, but there's a big city display tonight. We're all going to watch from the roof." Paige's eyes were glued to Tamsin as the alpha flowed through the kitchen, but the question was directed at Tory.

"I'm excited about the idea, but I'm heading into work after brunch. You'll have fun, there's no party like a pack party." Tory smiled softly. She loved her job but hated missing so much of the pack's comings and goings.

Paige finally wrenched her gaze from the woman she loved. "Wait, what? I thought tonight's celebration was a full pack thing. We watch fireworks together and then head out for a run. You won't be there? Does Tamsin know?"

Tory nodded. "It's my new job. I just got it. It's hard enough getting full moon nights off each month; getting all the holidays as well would be almost impossible. I don't think I'm working Tuesday, though. We'll probably run again, then."

Paige's face scrunched up. "Well, that sucks. Wait, no. I'm thrilled about Tuesday, but we'll miss you tonight. I'm glad you love your job, though, and that you're so good at it."

"I do, and I am." Tory smiled and held up her coffee mug in a silent salute.

A few hours later, Tory sat behind the nurses' station. There was a lull in emergencies for a couple of minutes.

"So, I sauntered up to this guy. His jeans were painted on him, a black long sleeve shirt hugging his muscles. I tell you, every part of me was at attention." Dwight leaned against the desk, a smirk on his face.

The rectangular station housed ten computers with enough room to work. On a normal night there were at most three to five people in the area at the time. Dwight, Tory, and Nia usually worked at one end. Their fearless leader, Dennis, tended to work at the other end, trying to focus when he could.

A pencil from behind hit the back of Dwight's head, and he laughed. Without turning, Dwight winked at Tory. "Are you jealous of my prowess, Dennis?"

A smile spreading on his face, Dennis crossed his arms behind his head and snorted. "Man, if I talked about the women I approached at bars the way you talk about the men you find, I'd be sent to HR. Do you even know the name of this guy you probably took home for a quick one night stand?"

Dwight's hand flew to his chest as his face morphed into a mask of horror. "A name? Good God, man! What do you take me for? That isn't what it was about. But we had a lot of fun, if you want any pointers."

Tory stood, ready to check on her patients. "No one needs your 'pointers,' Dwight. Literally. No one here cares. I'm starting to think your conquests are all in your head, my friend."

There was a round of snickers as everyone laughed and turned back to their computers.

Off to the side, Nia said, "I don't know. I could use some pointers on finding a hot guy. What can you tell me?"

With a smirk, Dwight let his eyes travel up and down her body before he said, "Easy, be gay."

Nia rolled her eyes then shook her head. Her blonde ponytail swung back and forth like a metronome. "You're incorrigible."

Tory looked at the other woman. She was an odd duck. Tory wasn't sure what it was about her, but they never quite got along despite Tory's efforts to be friendly. She was more into fashion than Tory as well, and wore fancy leather boots instead of practical shoes. Who did that? Sometimes, when Nia was nearby, the scent of old leather would make Tory wrinkle her nose.

"Agreed!" said Tory, sliding her arm into Nia's. "Let's—"

The phone for the ambulance rang. Tory stiffened, her senses on high alert. Leaning forward, Dennis snatched up the receiver. He relayed the information as he got it. "SUV crash. Five teens, two critical. Three minutes away."

All joking gone, the four ran to the doors to get to work.

None of the kids had been wearing seatbelts when the car they were driving took a turn too fast and rolled. Two had been thrown from the car before it had tumbled too far. Two had to be cut from the car with the jaws of life. The last was able to be dragged out of a door that still worked. No one thought they'd all survive. Tory wanted to save each and every one of them. She always did. *I became a nurse to save people.*

Tory assisted on one of the critical teens. The fifteen-year-old girl had been cut out of the front passenger seat of the car. She had lacerations on her head, arms, legs, and torso. Broken bones. Possible paralysis. That is, *if* she survived the night.

After hours of work, Tory and the doctor stepped back. The girl was somehow stable. Tory felt she'd fall on her face if she didn't get sleep soon.

The doctor looked at her. "You did good work, Byrd. With that blue hair and the fact that you look so young I wasn't sure, but you're a professional. Anytime I'm around, I'll happily work with you."

Tory gave him a small smile. She was used to being underestimated.

Nia came up and slid an arm around her shoulders. "You could take the blue out of your hair, you know." As nice as the gesture was, the words were condescending.

Tory bit back a sigh. "Then I'd just look twelve and most of the administrators would try to kick me out every time I walked into the building. I need something to remind people I work here."

She laughed. "Come on, let's get out of here. You look ready to drop."

They went and changed into their street clothes, then headed out. The night crew weaved through the people heading in. A few people gave nods and smiled, but most were too tired to do much more than trudge out.

It would be nice working days and having a regular schedule, but that usually came with a desk job. Tory shivered; she wouldn't be satisfied working with paper and not people. *Gah! All that paperwork!*

Chapter 2 - Release the Zombies
Mildred

A crowd of zombies shuffled from the hospital as Mildred made her way in. She watched the haggard nurses and doctors, and wondered what happened last night to keep them past their normal leaving time.

Why do I see a lot of paperwork in my future?

Among those in the crowd was the new hire—Toni? Tommy? Something. Her blue hair made Mildred smile every time she saw the petite woman zipping around the ER. Right now, she wasn't moving very fast; the woman dragged along with the rest of them.

Once in the hospital, Mildred zoned in on the coffee kiosk. The line wasn't long. "Your usual, Dr. Quincy?"

"Yes, please." She swiped her watch over the credit card machine and felt the vibration when the payment cleared.

Andy approached, tall and handsome, his normally sparkling blue eyes dull. Concern shot through Mildred. They'd been friends since childhood and had worked together since she'd gotten her job at the hospital. Like the doctors, he looked like he'd been in a boxing ring, and had lost. "Have you heard about last night in the ER, Mil?"

It must be bad, he usually starts with a little bit of a greeting.

"Morning, Andy." As the kiosk clerk handed her a tall cup of steaming coffee and a bag containing her pastries, Midred smiled her thanks. She turned towards the hallway, Andy following her. "No, I haven't. From the look of everyone heading out this morning, I imagine it was bad."

"An SUV rolled with five teens. Only two survived the night. We aren't sure if they'll make it 'til noon." His voice was drawn with stress.

A knot formed in Mildred's stomach, and she thanked her good fortune at not having sipped her coffee yet. "When do I need to speak with the parents? Are they available?"

"I've been working with them, but I need to go home soon. Let's move to your office, and I'll get you caught up on everything. We can meet with the parents in an hour. I convinced them to head to the cafeteria for food. We'll be notified if there's a change, but I doubt anything will happen for a few hours."

Relief flooded through her. Mondays were difficult enough. Transitioning from the weekend was always a process for Mildred. Having a few minutes to sort things out in her office helped. "Sounds good."

They started off talking about the crash before Andy moved on to the other cases so Mildred would be caught up for the day. He also wanted to hear about her weekend. They were friends, and he loved gossip.

They hadn't been talking for more than twenty minutes before her phone rang. Mildred checked the display and sighed. "Andy, it's my mother."

He winced. "Okay, I'll be back at eight-fifty."

She grimaced. "Thanks."

"Mother," she said in a level voice. She loved her family, but knew this wasn't going to go in a good direction. She watched as Andy shut her door on the way out. He mouthed, "Good luck," before he disappeared.

"Mildred, darling, did I tell you that your father and I went to Samantha's wedding last weekend?" Her voice sounded so light and pleasant, Mildred didn't trust it.

Mildred to a deep breath before answering. She needed to calm herself. "I know, Mother. I couldn't attend because I had a work meeting on Friday and couldn't drive down to Pasadena with you."

"That's right. The drive was lovely. We took the scenic route. The ocean is so beautiful. They had a fundraiser to save the forests and arboretums in the area. Did you know there's a lot of wildlife to try to keep safe?"

She stayed silent, knowing her mother wasn't done.

"It was so nice that Samantha followed her parents' lead. And that man her parents found, he was such a looker."

And there it is! How long until this becomes all about me and her expectations? She couldn't stop the annoyed sigh. *More coffee. I need more coffee.*

"I'm glad you had an enjoyable time, Mother. I'm really busy right now. Unless there's anything else, I really need to go." *Was that snappish? I need to focus, or she'll ask me what's wrong. I need to get her off the phone.*

"Mildred, darling, you haven't texted me back about the soiree on the fourth at the country club. You *will* be attending."

Mildred bit back her first response. "Is that a question? Because it didn't sound like one, and if it isn't, then that's why I didn't respond, Mother." She tried to keep the frustration from her voice. She knew she hadn't responded correctly as soon as the words were out of her mouth.

"Do not sass me, Mildred. You are thirty-two and haven't married. You are an embarrassment to me and your father. We sent you to excellent schools. University of California - San Francisco for your undergrad then Harvard University for your medical degree. You promised us once you found a job you'd let us help you find a husband, but you're still single."

She shook out her free hand once she realized her nails were cutting into her palm. "Maybe I don't want to date any of the people you've found. You don't understand the type of person I want to spend my time, and eventually, my life with, Mother."

"That's because you won't tell me."

Biting back a scream, Mildred took a deep breath. "Fine, Mother. I'll be at the country club at six tomorrow night. Okay?"

"Perfect. We have the perfect man for you. His name is Tanner. You'll love him."

Mildred wondered if there were any way to avoid the outing, the dinner, and the setup. She had nothing. "I really wish you hadn't done that."

"Until you start bringing your own dates, I'll continue providing ones for you."

Mildred wished she could explain to her mother, to her parents, why she never brought her own dates. Maybe one day she would, just to see her parents' faces, and to get it over with. Then she could live her own life without all these society events. "Goodbye, Mother."

And what, Mother, would you do, if I brought a woman to the country club? You'd freak out. You'd blow a gasket, is what you'd do.

Chapter 3 - Time to Stretch Your Legs
Tamsin

Tamsin walked around the alpha suite and its four rooms, if you counted the ensuite, while Paige got dressed for the day. She tallied what she could live with and what she wanted to change. Most of the area was similar to when her parents were alphas of the pack, but both her Uncle

Clyde and the clowns who followed him had made a few changes.

The master bedroom was fine, but the ensuite bathroom needed help ... a *lot* of help. She really wanted the den to meet the needs for when she had a stack of papers to grade, when she wanted to handle the business of the pack, and when Paige wanted a quiet place to write articles. As for the nursery, she wasn't ready to worry about that room yet. She had to fix the pack first.

Entering the nursery, she walked across the room and squatted down, pushing the small dresser away from the wall. She found the tiny heart with her name scrawled low to the floor from when she was—five? Six? No one had painted it in all these years. She smiled with the memory, tracing her younger self's writing.

With a sigh, she abandoned her assessment of the suite. The renovation must take the back-burner in favor of rebuilding her pack.

Tamsin headed towards the main floor. Descending the stairs, she saw the living room full of the people who trusted her to create a family here in Santa Cruz. On the far couch sat Jolly and Timothy watching their daughter Rainy. Their love infused the area. She smiled. *My hope is for there to be more kids in the pack. Hopefully more families will return.*

On the floor with Rainy was Joyce, mother of Blake. Blake was the newest wolf in the pack, and partner to Maria. Being the first wolf Tasmin had ever heard of who was also a witch, Blake would be an exciting addition to the pack.

From the kitchen, the scent of fish, rice, and vegetables permeated the air. Tamsin heard Orin and Connie, his wife, discussing the steps needed in cooking dinner. A third voice came from the room. *Is that Georgette helping in there?*

Behind her, she sensed a source of great love approaching just before Paige wrapped her arm around Tamsin's waist. "Are you going to finish walking down the stairs, love?"

"I'm just taking it all in. It's still all so new."

She could feel Paige's joy, as well as the emotions from the rest of her pack. "It's fantastic. Now, join me and the rest of our family."

"Not everyone. Tory couldn't get the night off, unfortunately."

"I know." Paige's arm tightened as she dragged Tamsin down the stairs. "But the full moon is next week, and she'll be with us then."

There were too many wolves to all shift and sneak out to their running ground together. They went out in twos and threes. Tamsin was in the last group with Paige and Georgette. They stripped, and Tamsin got on her hands and knees.

She recalled her first shift, back when she'd been eight years old. It took a while back then because her body didn't know what was happening. Over that first year, her body learned with each full moon. Now she could release her red wolf with a thought and a breath, even when the moon hid herself.

It still hurt. Everything moved. Bones changed shape. Hair retracted and regrew in other places. Nails were replaced with claws. Her whole body adjusted and reshaped. But it all occurred fast enough for Tamsin to ignore the pain and glory in the joy of becoming the wolf.

The explosion of fireworks brought her out of her memory. The city display was over, but that didn't stop people from setting them off around town. It hurt her ears. It was one of the reasons the pack wanted to get out into the wilderness.

Once her change was complete, she monitored the progress of Paige's white wolf and Georgette's gray. After they were all ready, they headed for the opening in the fence of the backyard. They darted down the trail, following the path they knew and the aroma of the others. Running felt amazing after the shift strained all her muscles.

The path from pack house to the woods passed by walkways frequented by many people. Tamsin could smell the regulars. Some of them had dogs who had escaped and found their trail, though their odor was a few days old. She scented the squirrels and feral cats; a few of the cats had a home in a fallen tree several minutes into their run.

She was tempted to stop and smell it all, but she knew she must present a good example as the alpha and restrain herself. The others would feel the same urge, and they all needed to move on to a safer spot. A pack of wolves sniffing the area would cause an uproar, and that would be bad. And so, they ran.

After running for ten minutes, they cleared the homes and she howled to the moon. The rest of the pack joined in, letting her know they passed the first gauntlet and made it to the end without being distracted.

Tamsin connected with the rest of her pack, and their joy resonated within her, everyone's pleasure—except for the one, dull spot belonging to Tory, stuck at work. Focusing on it for a moment, she could sense Tory was stressed. It wasn't beyond a normal night, but her packmate was busy. Tamsin didn't want to distract her, so she turned her full awareness to the world around her.

A yip ahead caught Tamsin's attention. Sniffing the air, Tamsin smelled a deer. With small signals to each of her wolves, Tamsin led her pack. They spread out. The hunt was on.

Blake and Maria took the left side. Orin and Connie flanked it on the right. After a few moments, Tamsin sent out a mental blast, *"Fall back, let her think she's pulling away."*

The pack slowed down, and the doe shot forward. Tamsin darted on a path parallel to the doe's and as she tired, Tamsin leaped, landing on the beast's back and taking her down.

As quickly as she could, Tamsin dispatched the doe. After taking a few bites as the alpha's prerogative, she signaled the rest.

Later, the pack ran to a stream, then headed back to pack house, excited about the successful hunt as a unit this Fourth of July.

Chapter 4 - Fireworks!
Mildred

Mildred walked around the emergency department taking note of staff, patients, and the flow of all the activity on the floor. It was a holiday, but the hospital never had a day off.

"Mildred?" She saw Tory, a few inches shorter than her, coming out of one of the curtained rooms. Her blue hair made her smile.

"Can I help you?"

"I know your shift ends in an hour, but my patient's transfer to the main hospital hasn't come. She needs to be admitted for observation. I don't want her stuck in the emergency department. Can you check into this before you leave? She's nervous and doesn't have family here." Once again, Tory's dedication to her patients impressed Mildred. She never let any of the people she worked with slip through the cracks.

She was an excellent hire.

As they spoke, nurses and doctors bustled around them. Despite the apparent chaos, Tory stayed focused on Mildred. With a smile, Mildred nodded. "I'll see what I can do."

"Thanks!" Before Mildred could blink, the other woman dashed off to her next patient.

Again, it's all about making sure everyone gets proper care. I'll need to make a note in her file when I get back to my office.

Dwight approached from the other direction. "We're running low on supplies in the supply closet. Andy said to tell you we needed a restock, stat."

She sighed, nodded, and headed to take inventory. Her day ended at eleven and she had enough work to last her a full eight hours. She dreamed about canceling on her family and just staying at the hospital instead of going to the country club for the Fourth of July celebration.

After her shower, Mildred sat on the edge of her bed glaring at her wardrobe. Every ounce of her being railed against playing dress-up to meet some man her mother thought was perfect for her. She knew if she didn't at least look presentable, then she'd embarrass her parents, and she didn't want to do that.

Slumping, she let out a long-suffering sigh, and pushed up from the bed. She found a light blue dress with thin, dark blue, vertical stripes. It buttoned in the front from the waist to her collarbone and had a matching light blue belt. It ended just past her knees. She found matching blue flats by the door. It was the perfect afternoon dress. She didn't hate it, but she'd be happier attending with the woman of her dreams.

For a moment, the image of the feisty, blue-haired Tory zipped through her mind. She'd never thought of the other woman as anything but someone who worked in her department. If she could find a woman with Tory's zeal and passion ... she shook her head. No, she had to focus on surviving a day at the country club, not imagining the perfect partner.

Mildred sighed again, grabbed her purse and phone, and headed out. The drive didn't take long. After she parked and walked through the club to the outside gathering area, she felt like she'd put on a new persona. Mildred Quincy, daughter of Albert and Priscilla Quincy, the leading money-managers in the area. They'd wanted Mildred to follow in their footsteps, but her heart had been in medicine. That wasn't the first way she'd disappointed them, and it wouldn't be the last.

She approached her family's table. Her mom had long brown wavy hair well past her shoulders. If you ignored that, they looked more like sisters than mother and daughter. Same high cheekbones, same brown eyes, same slender frame.

"Mildred, you made it. And don't you look lovely? That dress looks precious on you."

"Of course it does Mother. You picked it out."

Her mother wore a flowing flower-print dress with a wide-brimmed pink hat. Behind her, Mildred's father sat in a yellow button-down shirt that matched the flowers on her mother's dress. His hair had receded to a dark ring just above his ears, and his piercing blue eyes watched her.

Mother kissed each of Mildred's cheeks. "Tanner arrived just after your father and I did. He's been telling us stories of the pharmaceutical industry. The two of you will have so much to talk about."

Mildred clenched her jaw to stop herself from sighing. *Great! Just what I need, someone who wants to talk shop.* She couldn't believe this was the person her mother thought was a great match for her. She looked over Mother's shoulder and saw a tall, broad-shouldered man wearing sunglasses. His blond hair was perfectly sculpted, and his champagne suit looked tailored to his body.

He laughed at something her father said, then shot a glance over his shoulder to gaze at her. His smile widened, and he stood up. It didn't take his long legs more than two steps to eat up the distance between them, and he held out a wide hand to her. "Hello, Mildred. I'm Tanner; nice to meet you."

She shook his hand. "Nice to meet you, too." The cologne he wore rolled over her like a violent sandalwood wave. She normally liked the scent, but it was too much. It took all her manners to keep her smile of greeting from slipping. Years of training for the win!

"Your parents were telling me stories about you. A doctor? They're very proud."

The smile froze on her face. *I can only imagine what stories they've told you. Proud; I'm sure that's the word they used.* "Yeah, so I hear. And now they're trying to arrange something new to be proud of."

Tanner paused for a moment before laughing. His hand tightened on hers, and he gave a small tug. "Will you join me for a drink?"

She tried to make her smile genuine as she let him lead her to the table. "Why not?"

Before she could say anything more, he waved down the waiter. "Two strawberry margaritas, please."

She bit her bottom lip. It wasn't that she didn't like the margaritas here, it was just that she would have preferred if he'd asked what she wanted. *Is it worth arguing?* She sat and shook her head at her own questions. Her only goal was to survive the day.

He turned his million-dollar smile to her. "You're okay with a margarita, right?"

She blinked twice. "I guess so, since you ordered one." She didn't even try to modulate her tone. *I hope whomever he ends up with likes a controlling ass.*

She took a moment to look around the venue. There were over a dozen tables filled with people wearing jewel-toned dresses. Everyone looked happy: eating, drinking, talking, laughing. A small dance area was set up overlooking the ocean. There were two same-sex couples dancing. She knew gays were in their world, but being her parents' only child, she knew what the expectations were.

As she watched, a woman in a dress the same color as Tory's hair spun by with her partner. Mildred closed her eyes and imagined sitting with the other woman. She would've asked what Mildred wanted or, after a few dates, probably would know. They'd make a game out of guessing each other's orders. Laugh when they got it wrong.

Stop it, Mildred. You need to focus on the here and now, and not some nurse that works for you! She shook off the fantasy and took a calming breath. *At least they're playing decent music.*

"Excellent." Tanner's exuberant voice pulled her from her musings. It took her a second to remember he'd asked if she actually would *like* the drink he so rudely ordered for her. "So, you work at the hospital. That's fantastic. I'm new to the area; do you think you could ever give me a tour?"

"Are you asking as a pharmaceutical rep, or as a person new to the area interested in health care?" She widened her eyes, trying to make herself sound interested ... innocent even. *I wonder if it's working this time.*

"Oh." He leaned back. "I'm more interested as a person. We have underlings to try to sell the meds. Completely beneath my pay-grade, if you know what I mean." He waggled his eyebrows.

Mildred gave a bit of an artificial laugh, not that she thought he could tell the difference. "You know what? I just remembered something I have to ask my father. I'll be right back."

She got up and headed over to her parents. Mother's face lit up with joy. "Isn't he wonderful, Mildred?"

Her face scrunched up as she finally gave in to the emotions she felt. "He's awful, if you want to know the truth. Not one thing he's said has been anything but onerous. I can't stay here and be polite to him. I'm going to leave. Make an excuse; tell him I was called back to the hospital."

Father's face stiffened. "No. That's unacceptable, Mildred."

"So is this." She waved her hand. "All of this. It's like nails on a chalkboard. I'm done. Mother, I'll talk to you later, but right now, I'm leaving."

Walking away from the celebration was the best and worst feeling she'd had in a long time.

Chapter 5 - Everyone Deserves Care
Tory

The machine next to Tory beeped as it monitored the vitals of the older woman lying in the bed next to her. The woman was in her late sixties and looked withered from years of smoking. Tory continued to fill out the basic questionnaire that came up on the electronic medical record.

"How long have you been experiencing these symptoms?"

The woman, Hazel, coughed a few times, dry barking coughs. They weren't the kind of cough that meant cold or flu; they meant weak lungs.

"Longer than you've been alive, sweetie." She squinted at Tory. "What are you, twelve?"

Tory chuckled. "So, twelve years?" She made as if to type on the computer.

Hazel barked out a laugh. "Oh, I like you. I was diagnosed with COPD twenty years ago. I immediately stopped smoking. I'd like to see you give up a lifetime addiction from a single diagnosis! But if you're talking about what brought me in tonight, the symptoms started yesterday."

The doctor came in and gave Hazel a charming smile. She came and looked over Tory's shoulder. "Symptoms for just over twenty-four hours. The vitals look good. Byrd, I know how busy you are. Are you done with your questions?"

Tory nodded. "I am. If you don't need me, I'll head out."

"Sounds good."

Tory ducked out and headed to the nurse's station. Dwight stood staring at the schedule. As she approached, he shot a look at her. "Tory! Perfect. Exactly who I wanted to see."

One of her eyebrows shot up. "Oh? Really?"

"You know you're my favorite."

She shook her head. "I seriously doubt that, but I'll bite. What do you want, my friend?"

He winked at her. "You're scheduled for Friday. I'm here on Saturday. Can we swap? I have this seriously hot date. I'd owe you." He widened his dark brown eyes, giving her his most pitiful puppy-dog look.

Tory rubbed her eyes. In reality, she didn't care. She never had a 'hot date' and one night was much the same as another, save the full moon nights. As she thought about dating someone, Mildred's face floated through her mind. Gah! Like dating was ever going to happen. Dating her sexy boss was very much out of the question.

She wasn't scheduled for the full moon this month, but it could easily happen in the future. Building bridges now could only help in the future.

"Sure." She dropped her hands and nodded. "We can switch."

Eyes bright, he swung around and gave her a hug. "Thank you, doll. You're the best!"

Before either of them could say anything else, the emergency phone rang. Ambulance coming in.

"I got it," Tory said.

She headed to meet the ambulance.

"We were called over to that homeless encampment. White male. We're estimating in his late fifties."

"Estimating? No ID?" Tory watched as the EMTs pulled the man from the ambulance.

"No identification. Homeless man. He said he can't remember his age. All he said was: 'old as dirt.'"

Tory took the report while they rolled the gurney towards a room, navigating around other nurses and equipment in the hall. "What were the symptoms?"

"Coughing, shortness of breath, sharp and sudden chest pain, dizziness. He thought it was a heart attack."

Tory started shaking her head, a few ideas crystalizing. "Any leg pain or swelling?"

The man grunted. "Some pain. Don't know if my leg is swollen." He started to cough and rub his chest after he spoke. A bit of blood came out with his cough.

As they rolled him into a room, Tory called to Dwight. "Get me Dr. Aimes. Tell him this is priority one." *Please understand this means life or death.*

By the time they'd shifted the homeless man to the emergency room bed and the EMT were rolling the stretcher out, Dr. Aimes ran in. "Report."

Tory gave a run down of what she'd learned. "My thoughts are pulmonary embolism."

The doctor hardly paused for a moment, taking in all the information. "Yes. I concur." Before they could do more, the man began to cough again and then deflated on the table. "Paddles."

Despite trying to save him, nothing they did helped. Dr. Aimes looked at the clock. "Time of death: one forty-three a.m."

With a heavy heart, Tory headed to the nurse's station to fill out her report.

Chapter 6 - Dot Your 'I's and Cross Your 'T's
Mildred

The alarm went off and Mildred wanted nothing more than to roll over and go back to sleep. She'd stayed up too late the night before reading a book and now she'd paid for it. Sometimes her morning self really hated her night self.

Normally, she didn't hit the snooze on her alarm, but this morning she needed the extra eight minutes in bed ... and another eight minutes. And ... crap! She leapt from bed and threw on some clothes.

Her stomach growled as she tied her shoes. *Damn it! I need food and don't have time.* She checked her watch. *Café! I'll go to the café.*

The drive to The Zesty Bean only took a few minutes. She ran in. There were only three people ahead of her when she got in line. It didn't take long to get to the barista. She ordered a breakfast sandwich and a large latte. Once she had the bag and cup, she zipped back to her car and made it to work in record time.

She decided to do a quick walk-through of the emergency room to see if there was anything she needed to be aware of. One of the nurses coming out of a room caught her attention, the blue hair a shocking bright spot in the sea of blondes, brunettes, and redheads.

Mildred made a bee-line towards Tory while pulling out her phone to check her assumption. *Should she be here?* The verification didn't take long. "Tory!" She called out.

Tory's head popped up, though the woman looked tired. "Mildred, morning. Can I help you?"

"I was just curious why you're here now. According to my schedule, you should be here tonight, not now."

Her brows rose, forcing her eyes to open wider. "Ah, that. I swapped nights with Dwight."

"Why didn't you put it into the system?" *Are they trying to hide something? Of course, they aren't.*

A streak of annoyance shot through Mildred. This situation wasn't helped by her lack of sleep. Narrowing her eyes, she thought back to hiring the young-looking Tory with the crazy blue hair. She hadn't done many reviews of the new hire. *Was she the right choice for the job if she couldn't follow such a simple procedure?* She shook her head. She knew the nurse was excellent with patients. She could be trained ... right?

Tory opened her mouth to answer, but Mildred waved her off. "Never mind. We'll talk later. Next time you do a swap, talk to me first."

With a dumbfounded or maybe an annoyed look, Tory turned and walked towards another room.

Mildred went to her office to eat and check over paperwork. Still frustrated and distracted with too many thoughts, she decided to head down to the main floor, do rounds, and observe the staff.

Behind the nurses' desk, Dennis and Nia bantered about their Fourth of July hijinks, only adding to Mildred's annoyance. She didn't want to be reminded of that day and her awful 'date.'

On a whim, she poked her head into the staff's lounge and saw Tory resting on a couch. Her eyes were closed, and her skin looked pale. *Is that the lighting in here? How long has she been lazing about? Isn't her shift over in a couple of hours? Is a long break really called for now?*

"Tory, shouldn't you be on the floor right now? You're off soon. Why are you in here now?"

With a grunt, the woman pushed herself up. "Sorry. I'm heading back out now."

Mildred watched her go. The normally zippy nurse trudged from the room and headed towards a patient. Mildred took a moment to wonder if she was coming down with something. She needed to find out before a member of staff needed an extended amount of time off.

Back at the nurse's station, only Dennis was left. "Kind of harsh on her, don't you think?"

"She's off soon. Do you think she needs to be sleeping right now?" Mildred straightened some papers on the counter. She started to second-guess her assumptions. She trusted Dennis, and he rarely called her out.

Dennis gazed at her with a blank face, then started speaking in a matter-of-fact voice. "A woman came in at one a.m. with a broken arm. Tory kept her calm while it was properly set. Then stayed with her until she was sedated. As soon as she was taken to surgery, a girl came in throwing up. Nia asked Tory to take it because she was about to take a meal break." He shook his head. "Nia was just avoiding the smell, if you ask me." His mouth tightened for a moment before he sighed. "Tory was about to take her first fifteen-minute break when you told her to get back out there."

Mildred gaped at him. "Why didn't she tell me?"

"Give her boss excuses?" Dennis shrugged. "She wouldn't."

Chapter 7 - Two is Not a Pattern
Tory

Tory headed out to the waiting room. "Mark Eshton," she called.

A boy in a wheelchair surrounded by adults looked up. He wore a karate gi. His face was a mask of pain, but he tried to hide it. One of the adults, tall and fit, with short blond hair, stood and pushed him towards her.

"I can take over if you want," she offered.

"Nah, I got it. Lead on." His voice was low and solemn.

They headed back to one of the exam rooms. "Mark, are you okay answering questions in front of this adult?"

Mark sniffed once. "He's my dad, so yeah, it's fine."

Tory nodded. "Perfect." She checked his vitals and medical background. Once done, she moved on to questions about what happened. "It sounds like you may have broken your leg. Things can be slow around here at night. I'm going to go ahead and order an X-ray. The technician will bring the mobile unit around, though it may take an hour or so. Hopefully the doctor will be in before that happens, but if not, I just want to expedite your night."

The dad slumped. "Thank you. We waited almost an hour to get into the room. I was afraid we'd be here until sunrise."

Tory smiled. "I'm often here that long, but without my excuse, I agree, it isn't the best way to spend your time. If you have any questions, the nurses station is just outside these doors. There's usually someone there."

The man squinted at her nametag. "Byrd. Okay, I'll ask for you if I need anything. Thank you, ma'am."

"Not a problem." She gave the two a smile as she left the room.

Out at the nurses station, she logged into a computer to finalize her notes. Dwight walked up. "Heya Tory, I heard you got in trouble for our swap last weekend."

"Nothing big. I didn't realize we needed to put it into the computer. Lesson learned."

His chin dropped and eyebrows shot up. "She yelled at you."

"She didn't yell."

"Fine. A reprimand."

Tory opened her mouth to argue, but Dwight held up his hands. "Listen, she's our boss. If you weren't trained, that's on her. Yes, I could've put in the swap, but you're so organized I just assumed you'd done it."

Tory barked out a laugh. "That's some excuse. I'll make sure to tell Mildred that next time. It wasn't done because I'm *too* organized." She shook her head.

"Mildred? Not Dr. Quincy?" Dwight leaned in closer.

Tory shook her head. "What, doesn't everyone call each other by their first names around here?"

"Yes, but there was something in the way you said her name." His eyes narrowed. "I am an excellent judge of character, did you know that?" His chin lifted as he rubbed it with thumb and finger. "My God ... you like her."

"As a boss? Sure, why not? She's mostly been great."

Dwight's brow rose. "Oh, no, Tory. You know what I mean. Why didn't I see this before? Why has my gaydar been on the fritz around you? You are interested in our fearless leader."

"What?" Tory hadn't even thought about Mildred that way. Sure, the woman was beautiful, and when she wasn't being prickly, seemed quirky and fun. She liked her. But *like* like? "I don't know what you're talking about."

A Cheshire cat smile took over Dwight's face. "Oh, but you will, my dear. You will." He turned and sauntered into one of the waiting rooms.

Tory shook her head. *I'm glad that man isn't a witch with premonitions. That would be just too scary!*

The phone for an ambulance rang, and Tory headed for the bay after getting the time of arrival. A homeless man. Once in the room, it became clear it was a pulmonary embolism. They kept him alive for thirty-seven minutes before he died. Back at her station, Tory realized this patient was similar to one she'd had before. The stats were almost identical to last time, except this time the man was younger, maybe in his forties.

What are the chances that two homeless men would come in with a pulmonary embolism? This can't be a coincidence.

Before she could talk to anyone, another ambulance brought a woman with whiplash. Once Tory checked the woman in, documented her medical background and vital statistics, she handed her off to the doctor and went to check on the karate kid.

"How's my favorite patient?" she asked with a wide smile.

Mark looked up, face pasty white. "I'm fine. I was supposed to test for my black belt this summer. Do you think I'll be able to do that?"

Tory clenched her jaw and tried to keep a blank face. "Has the X-ray technician come in yet?"

Mark's father nodded. "You just missed him. He said the official reading will take another hour."

The door opened and Dr. Aimes walked in. He shot Tory a quick look before all his focus was on Mark. "How are you doing tonight?"

It took Mark a moment to answer. "It's my leg. I just want to be able to do karate."

Dr. Aimes smiled at Tory. "You're welcome to stay, but if you're busy, I'll fill you in once I'm done here."

She nodded and headed out. Selecting the next person in the waiting room, she found another kid. *Not a good night to be a kid in Santa Cruz!* A teen who smashed her thumb in the car door when she got out. Her boyfriend brought her in, a man a bit older than her.

"I'd like to speak with just—" Tory gazed back down at the paperwork, "—Neveah, please."

The boyfriend's face twisted, and he was about to say something, but Tory let out a bit of her werewolf dominance. She didn't do it often, but in a situation like this, it helped. "You aren't family. After the initial examination, if Neveah wants you with her, then I'll come get you. For now, please wait here."

Eyes wide, the boyfriend's mouth snapped shut and he glared at her.

The two walked back, and Tory watched Neveah's hands tremble as they got further and further from the boyfriend, though she tried to hide it. Tory could smell the underlying fear on the woman.

In the room, Tory found an ice pack for the girl and then opened up an extra questionnaire. "Do you feel safe in your current situation?"

"Um ... what?"

"You heard me. Do you feel safe?"

Hands clasped in her lap holding the ice back on her injury, Neveah held herself as still as she could. *She looks like prey.* "I did this to myself. It was an accident when I shut the car door."

"Okay. These questions will only take a moment."

Neveah breathed in a shaky breath. "He's a good man. He takes care of me."

The check-in took longer than usual. Neveah wouldn't speak poorly about her boyfriend. After that, she finished the regular check in, and returned to the nurses station. The whole situation made Tory feel dirty. She could smell the lies the girl spoke, but couldn't call her out. It wouldn't help the situation. Her hands were tied.

Dr. Aimes approached the desk. "I'm done with Mark in room six. He needs crutches for his broken leg and a demonstration on how to use them. Then you can roll him out. I'm heading in to see the patient with the crushed finger. Anything I should know about her?"

Tory had so much she wanted to say, but didn't. "I'm not sure. Her boyfriend seems ... rough, but she hasn't said anything negative about him."

The doctor nodded. "I'll see what I can figure out."

She nodded. "Good. One more thing before you head in there ... do you think it's odd that we've had two homeless people come in two weeks with a pulmonary embolism? Like, isn't that weird?"

He tilted his head. "Maybe, but two cases doesn't mean much. Don't see something where there's nothing to see, Byrd." He swept away into Neveah's room.

She checked over her notes and saw a message pop up on her screen. The woman with whiplash was ready to be released. She grabbed the paperwork and headed into her room.

Back at the nurses station, she saw she only had a half hour before she could go home. She was exhausted down to her bones. All she wanted to do was sleep.

An ambulance came with an old man who'd collapsed. Nia was up. She ran over to Tory. "Can you take this one? Please? I'll owe you. I just can't with another old man. We can switch with the girl with the crushed finger."

Tory rubbed her eyes. Neveah would be discharged within the hour. That man would be here for hours. "Nia, I'm out of here soon. My shift is pretty much over. Talk with Dennis. He just started."

Nia's face hardened. "Right. You'll swap with Dwight, but not me. Got it."

Before Tory could say anything else, Nia stomped away.

Too tired to think, Tory waited for the discharge order to come ... for Neveah ... for herself. It was time.

Chapter 8 - Complaints, Morning 'til Sundown
Mildred

On Wednesday, Mildred had barely sat down with her coffee and pastry when someone knocked on her door. "Come in."

A bedraggled looking Nia entered. It was the end of the woman's shift, and she dragged her way in and flopped onto one of Mildred's chairs. "Do you have a minute to talk before I head home?"

"Of course. How can I help you?"

Nia's shoulders slumped and she gazed down at her hands. "I just, well, I don't want to get anyone in trouble, it's just ... I want to talk to you about Tory."

Mildred laced her fingers on her desk and smiled at the other woman, welcoming her to speak. She'd grown up around rich kids who got their way. She'd watched as her friends and nonfriends manipulated the adults around her. She wasn't sure why Nia's performance brought back the private school antics, but something about how the woman came in, sat, and showed fake concern did. She knew she shouldn't downplay a complaint, but everything in her screamed to tread lightly. "Tell me what happened."

Taking a deep breath, Nia nodded quickly. Her eyes were wide, and she drew her bottom lip into her mouth before she spoke. "It may be nothing, but last night I asked her to swap patients with me. You know, we do that sometimes. An ambulance was about to arrive, and Tory had a patient in room nine—not that that matters." She shook her head. "Anyway, I asked if she could swap. Her patient was a girl I thought may be being abused, and I didn't think Tory was taking it seriously enough. I wanted to help out. She snapped at me, loud enough for patients to hear. It was completely unprofessional."

Mildred tilted her head. Nothing that she'd seen or heard from the blue-haired beauty matched what Nia said. Tory had always seemed the height of professional. She waited for Nia to say more. When the pause went on longer than expected, she asked, "Did anyone say anything about it?"

Nia's brow furrowed. "Um, no ... well, yes. One patient mentioned it to me. He said Tory seemed so young. I mean, what is she, like, twenty-four?"

The question was not pertinent to their conversation. Mildred ignored it. "What did you say to this patient?"

"Oh, I just said not to worry; everything was fine."

"Did any of the other nurses or doctors overhear this exchange you had with Tory?"

Her mouth pursed as she thought. "I don't think so. Anyway, I just thought you should know." She dropped her voice to a loud whisper, like there was someone else in the office. This woman was all about the gossip. *Stop judging people! Why am I so protective of Tory?* "I don't think she's really a team player, and I know that's something you really pride yourself on here."

Mildred took out a pad of paper and jotted down some notes. She'd have to look into this. From what she could remember, Tory had been helping out more than her share, and she'd never known Nia to step up to help anyone, but she'd need to speak with Dennis. He was lead and knew the work relationships better than anyone.

"Is there anything else, Nia?"

The nurse shook her head, then perked up. "I think she may be inexperienced, you know, being so young and all. I just worry for our patients and the care we give."

"Okay, I'll take all of this under advisement. Thank you, Nia. Have a good rest."

The woman pushed herself up slowly and trudged from the room. Just as Mildred was about to call Dennis in, her phone rang. Eight-thirty, on the nose, every time!

She pasted a smile on her face. "Hello, Mother. How can I help you this morning?"

"Mildred, darling, I just wanted to remind you that you agreed to come to dinner with me and your father this Saturday."

"Of course, I remember. I assume your normal table at Ocean Sunrise?"

"There isn't a better restaurant in town dear. Where else would we go? The chef has put together a seven course tasting menu paired with Sonoma County wines. It's guaranteed to be a delight. We've arranged a date for you, so dress especially nice, darling."

Mildred was about to argue when Dr. Aimes appeared in her doorway. His face was tight and eyes hard. *What now?* With a sigh, Mildred said, "That's fine, Mother. I'll see you on Saturday at seven-thirty." She got off the phone and waved the good doctor in.

She wondered if she'd ever get to her regular work or if there was a line of people outside her office just waiting to speak with her.

Chapter 9 - Howling to The Moon
Tory

Tory sat in the living room, enjoying the mayhem of being in the middle of her pack. Young Rainy had an explosion of toys around her. Joyce was playing with her. Jolly and Timothy sat on a couch opposite Tory, watching their daughter. Or, more accurately, Timothy watched while Jolly played on her phone. Maria and Blake sat together, discussing Maria's day. The rest were in the kitchen making a feast fit for ... well, a pack of wolves.

Georgette walked out of the kitchen and dropped down next to Tory on a couch. "Tell me a story about your work."

A smile split Tory's face. Georgette always wanted to hear about her day-to-day dramas. They spent a few minutes talking about crazy life in the ER.

Tory smiled. "We had this one man in. He couldn't get his blood sugar numbers down. He came in early and had two daughters and three sons who cycle in to visit him."

Georgette's eyes sparkled. "Were any of the others diabetic? Was it a family condition?"

"It was, but I only know because as I was in and out, some of them told me. They said they knew what their dad was going through, and almost all of the kids said they wanted to bring him home. 'Why does he have to stay here? I have diabetes, I know how to help him eat to maintain better health. Staying here just depletes our savings.' It wasn't like there was anything I could do."

Shaking her head, Georgette smiled. "How long was he there?"

"It felt like hours." Tory leaned back. "After the third test, his numbers got worse. It shouldn't have been possible."

"Gods above, what did you do?"

"We watched. They all knew I was his nurse, but despite Dwight's obnoxiousness, he can be stealthy. He and Dennis stationed themselves so that one of them could always keep an eye on the room. They saw when one of the kids snuck a chocolate bar to his dad. When I went in to ask her about it, she said one couldn't hurt. After several questions, it turned out *all* of his kids had the same thought. Their dad was in the emergency department for a blood sugar level over four hundred, and they were all sneaking him more sugar. I tell you, with family like that ..."

Orin came out and called them all to dinner. The cooks outdid themselves: three full baked salmon, new potatoes with herbs and butter, a salad, asparagus, rolls, and caramel cupcakes filled with vanilla chocolate chip buttercream for dessert. Everyone was silent for the first few minutes, enjoying the feast.

Tamsin sighed. "Everything is excellent as always."

Next to her, Paige grinned. "I helped with the potatoes."

Tory speared at one with a fork. "What did you do? Cut them in half? Help with the roasting?"

Paige chuckled. "Gods, no! I washed them, and even that was tricky in the start. Kitchening is almost as scary as taking down big game!"

Tory laughed and ate another bite of potato. "Well, you did an excellent job. They're delicious."

Paige beamed. "Why, thank you."

At the other end, Orin shook his head. "I think Paige could burn hard boiled eggs."

Tory nodded sagely. "I did that once."

Paige laughed at the joke, but Orin sighed. "I remember. The house stank for days. Why do you think we kick you out of the kitchen so often?"

Across from them, Blake's eyes narrowed. "You've got to be joking. How do you *burn* hard boiled eggs?"

Georgette snorted. "You forget you're boiling them until the sulfur scent takes over the house."

Tory shrugged. "I got caught up in a movie."

Tamsin chuckled. "My parents banned you from the kitchen for a month, if I remember correctly."

"Three months. But Connie had to cook for all of us after that, and look where it got her." Tory leaned forward to look at the woman who ran the kitchen of the hottest restaurant in town, Ocean Sunrise. "You're welcome, by the way."

A bun hit her head as she leaned back, and everyone laughed.

When her plate was almost cleaned off, her phone buzzed. Tory pulled it out and saw it was a call from Dwight. "I'm going to take this." She waved her phone.

Tamsin nodded. "Be ready in fifteen."

Nodding, Tory tapped her phone. "Hey, what's up?"

The sounds of the hospital could be heard in the background. Though she thought he must be covering the microphone, she could still hear talking in the background. "Okay. I just spoke with Dennis, who had a meeting with Mildred. Remember, you didn't get this from me. Apparently, Nia went and complained about you because you didn't swap patients with her the other night."

Tory pinched the bridge of her nose in annoyance. "Really? I never thought she'd be so petty. What was there to complain about?"

"She made up some stuff about you yelling at her and a patient complaining."

Tory's heart began to pound harder in her chest and chills washed through her. "She said what?"

"Don't worry. As it goes, I was in the room across from the nurses station and heard the whole exchange. I told Dennis the real story. But be careful of her, okay?"

"Yeah. It's just, wow. I thought she was my friend ... or at least a professional."

"I'm your friend. Dennis is your friend. Remember that." He paused and she heard the sound of an alarm and the clatter of a cart. "Look, I have patients, I have to go. I'll see you later this week."

Once off the phone, Tory wanted to scream. This was the real world, not middle school. She couldn't believe what Dwight had told her. She'd have to talk to Dennis about it ... she just had to figure out a stealthy way to bring it up.

She gave herself a few minutes to calm down before heading outside to shift for her full moon run. If she thought she'd needed it before, then she really needed it now.

Tamsin gazed at her, concern in her eyes. "Tory, Maria, Blake. Shift first, and head out."

Tearing off her clothes, Tory let her wolf out. The pain was a welcome diversion. Once she saw the other two were ready, she darted out, speeding down the trail. None of the others moved as fast as she did. It didn't matter, they'd all end up in the same place, and she needed to move, release her frustration, and howl out her anger.

"Peace, my friend. I don't know what happened, but don't go off alone. Let the pack help you." Tamsin's voice came to her, centering Tory with the pack. She barely realized she'd made it to the meeting spot and had been ready to tear away, running to escape her thoughts. Standing to wait, she smelled the eucalyptus trees, and debated getting something with that scent to help bring her peace on trying nights. She paced with too much energy to stand still, the moist ground spongy under her paws. In an effort to stop her tumbling thoughts, she went to investigate a bush with a luscious-smelling flower.

Hearing others approach, Tory moved from the greenery and howled to the mother moon, a lonely sound that would bring sadness to any who heard it.

Chapter 10 - Wrapping up Loose Ends
Mildred

"Your regular, Dr. Quincy?"

"Yes, please." She waved her watch over the credit card box and waited for the vibration to inform her she'd paid.

She watched as the barista in charge of the kiosk quickly made a large coffee with a splash of cream and a dash of sugar. The woman put a blueberry muffin in a bag and handed everything over. "Have an excellent day!"

Despite it being a Monday, Mildred was hopeful for the week. "Thank you."

Turning away and heading towards the elevator, she ran into Andy. "Good morning, Andy. How are you this fine Monday? Was the weekend as insane as always?"

He threw back his head and laughed. "Of course! Probably as crazy as your weekend with your parents. How was the latest date?"

She groaned. "Please don't remind me. I was just feeling good about today! Every time. At least this time he didn't try to get his pharmaceutical company's foot in the door here."

"Oh, no. Really?"

They'd reached her office and she dropped into her seat. She massaged her temples. "I forgot I didn't tell you about that. Yep, that was the last one. They're really getting to the bottom of the barrel, I tell you. Just awful."

"Can you tell your parents to stop setting you up?" She saw real concern in his face, heard it in his voice.

"I've tried. Unless I have a ring on my finger, they won't listen."

"You know, there are a lot of vendors down on the wharf that sell rings. I'm sure you could get a great deal on one."

Mildred slapped her hand over her mouth as she snorted. "Can you imagine? I'll just tell them my partner is always busy."

"I'm sure that'll be just fine. Your parents seem very chill about all things you and dating. Put on a ring, it'll be enough."

Mildred tried to stop laughing so she could drink her coffee, but the whole conversation was so ridiculous, and Adam kept making it worse. She finally caught her breath. "Okay, enough. I'll figure something out eventually. Anything else happen this weekend I should know about?"

"Nah." He said, a wide grin on his face. "All the crazy happened last Thursday for the full moon. Once we survived that, the weekend was almost a vacation."

They spent a few minutes covering his notes before he left. Mildred ate her muffin and reviewed what she wanted to accomplish for the day. As she shuffled some papers around, she found the note she'd written about Nia complaining about Tory. *I need to look into this. I'll spend some time this afternoon doing rounds and observing everyone in the ER.*

Decision made, Mildred got down to wrangling the other paperwork she needed to clear away.

An hour after lunch, Mildred headed down to the ER. She checked in with Dennis to let him know she would be around if he needed anything. Though she was there to observe all the staff, she made sure to focus on Tory.

A woman in an expensive suit came in with a rash. Tory was efficient and respectful—exactly what was expected.

An hour later, walking down the hall, Mildred saw Tory focused on a computer, entering data. Another nurse tapped her on the shoulder to ask a question about a patient's symptoms. Tory closed her eyes for a moment before giving her opinion. "But check with Dennis. He had a patient with similar symptoms last week, and he's more knowledgeable about this than I am."

Mildred was impressed with both her quick answer and her willingness to admit others may know more than her. Before she could move on, another nurse, newly hired, came up to ask Tory a procedural question.

Tory laughed. "I know, right? It took me a couple of days to get this all figured out. Let me show you, and feel free to re-ask any time you want. I get it."

An ambulance came in, and Tory dashed off. Nia approached the new nurse with a smile. "You can ask me anything, too, you know. I've been here longer. Tory is pretty new, so she isn't that good with all of this yet."

The new-hire just stared at Nia, uncertain. "Is what Tory told me wrong?"

"Well, no. Not *this* time."

The nurse shrugged. "It wasn't last time either. But thanks, I'll consider coming to you instead."

"You should. I really know my way around here."

Mildred just stayed tucked away, watching as the new-hire darted off to the room of one of her patients. Nia headed off and found another nurse sitting at the nurse's station and began gossiping.

As they spoke, Tory dashed by with a man on a stretcher. "Nia, I need the doctor in room four, priority one."

Nia looked up at her and gave a curt nod. She broke off from her gossiping to get to work. Mildred followed the drama to room four.

Dr. Aimes came in. "Talk to me, Byrd."

A genuine smile lit up Tory's face and it stole Mildred's breath for a moment. Then the moment passed as Tory got down town to business. The smile shifted to a mask of concern. "It's another one, sir. Same symptoms and from the same location. This makes three. Do we call it a pattern yet?"

The doctor jumped in. "Another pulmonary embolism? You're kidding?"

"I wish I was. It's like there's something in the water over at the homeless encampment."

While they spoke, the two worked diligently. Tory showed the same respect she did for the obviously wealthy woman. Despite everything they tried, the homeless man didn't survive.

Mildred decided to do one more round before heading back to her office. When she passed the nurses station, Dwight waggled his eyebrows at Tory. "Can we swap again?"

Tory sighed overly dramatically. "Another big date? Same man or another no-name heart-stopper?"

"You know I never remember their names. I am too young to commit to one person."

This time Tory laughed. "Fine, we can switch. You know my schedule isn't nearly as in demand as yours. Let me get it into the computer before either of us forget."

"Thanks! You're a doll."

On the way to the elevator, Mildred spotted Dennis. "Do you have a minute?"

"Sure. But only just. We seem to be very busy for a Monday. This weekend must've been the calm before the storm."

"I got a complaint that Tory yelled at Nia. I mentioned this to you before. Did you follow up?"

"I did. I couldn't find any proof of her accusation. Actually, I found someone who heard the conversation, and said it went down very differently. I don't want to get anyone in trouble, but I really don't think Tory should be getting any reprimand."

Mildred nodded. "I'm starting to think the same. Thank you."

"Not a problem." She turned to head back to her office. She had enough information and needed to get back to the stacks of paperwork and a ten o'clock meeting.

I'm not sure why Nia complained about Tory, or what she has against the other woman. All I know is, I should probably keep an eye on the situation.

Chapter 11 - Time Keeps On Slipping ... Into the Future
Tory

The buzz in the emergency room faded to the background as Tory hobbled to the nurse's station. She knew she hadn't been working for over twenty-four hours, but it kind of felt like it. She couldn't believe it was September and she'd been back in Santa Cruz for four months and had this job for three. Time had flown, but it also felt like she'd worked here forever.

Sitting at one of the computers, Dwight looked up at her and gave her a wide smile. "Girl, you look ready to fall over. When do you go home?"

"Not soon enough!" she groused. Looking around, she realized it was just the two of them. She'd been wanting to discuss her theory with him, but there were always others around. "Hey, can I ask you a question?"

"Sure. Is it about how I have so many fabulous dates?" He waggled his eyebrows at her.

"Um ... no." She chuckled. "In the last two months, since early July, we've had six homeless people with pulmonary embolisms. They've all come from that same encampment. Don't you think that's strange? Something we should take notice of?"

"You know there's drugs and alcohol in those encampments, Tory."

Her lips twitched. "That doesn't explain it. Look at my records. It's more than that."

"Tory!"

"Dwight!"

Dwight shook his head. "You're obsessed, you know that, right? It's a fluke, it doesn't mean anything. You're seeing things where there isn't anything to be seen."

She rubbed her face. "I was thinking about taking this to Mildred. See if she noticed anything."

"Don't. Focus on your job. Things have been going well for you. Why rock the boat?"

Tory slumped. "I guess. I just ... fine. I guess you're right."

Nia swung in. "Dwight's right? Put it on the calendar. We should have a party."

"Ha. Ha." Dwight rolled his eyes.

Nia winked. "So, Dwight. Hot date Friday night? Tory? Do *you* have a date? Wait, you never have a date." She grabbed her belly, threw her head back, and laughed. Neither Tory nor Dwight laughed with her. *What did I ever do to her? Bitch.* "Anyway, I *do* have a date on Friday and need a swap. Either of you available?"

Tory thought about it, and realized she already worked Friday. She was about to say something when Dwight said, "Not me, I'm busy Friday. Sorry, friend."

Nia's face dropped. "Of course you are. Always busy." Before Tory could give an answer, Nia turned to her. "And my guess is, you won't swap because you only swap with Dwight. You're never willing to swap with me. Why? Am I not good enough?"

Before Tory could answer, Nia spun on her heel and stormed away, mumbling under her breath.

Dwight glared after her. "She never let you answer." He pulled up the schedule on his phone. "You already work Friday. Do you think she even checked before she snapped at you?"

"Nope, she just expected the worst." Tory took a deep breath. Okay, I'm going to head back to work. Break's over.

They both stood as the phone call came that an ambulance was coming in.

Tory shook out her arms, trying to find a second—third?—wind. "I got it. You get the next one from the waiting area."

As the EMTs pulled the man out of their vehicle, they started to call out information. "Homeless woman, fifty-two. Pain in her left arm and chest."

As they rolled the woman to the room, Tory gaped as her assumptions were proven wrong. "A heart-attack? Does she come from the encampment?"

"Yes."

She spied a nurse at the nurse's station. "Call in a code one."

Dr. Aimes came in a moment later. "Another pulmonary embolism?"

"No, heart attack."

He paused for a moment before jumping in. They worked hard to save the woman, and in the end, she survived.

Unfortunately, the next one didn't.

Chapter 12 - A Picture is Worth a Thousand Shots
Mildred

The traffic was thick as Mildred navigated the roads to the hospital. She hoped parking wouldn't be too bad. All she could think about was a large coffee and a sweet blueberry muffin. She didn't always indulge ... well, maybe she did, but the hospital kiosk bought their muffins from a local bakery, and they were delicious.

Her mouth watered just thinking about the tasty treat. She knew she should be thinking about all the work on her desk, but she wanted a few more minutes of solitude—

A vibration in her pocket ... a phone call.

The car's display told her it was her mother. Mildred toyed with the idea of letting the call go to voicemail, but ... it was her mother. After taking a deep breath, and exhaling any tension she held, she answered the call. "Hello, Mother. It's a bit early for you to be calling, isn't it?"

"Mildred, darling, I have a class at eight o'clock this morning. Can you imagine? Who schedules classes that early? Who does anything that early?"

"A lot of people," Mildred mumbled. She wanted to bang her head. "Again, Mother, is there a reason you called?"

"Oh, yes, of course. Though I don't know why I need a reason to call." She chuckled. "There is an end-of-summer event at your aunt's gallery this Saturday. I am hoping you will find time in your busy schedule to join us."

It was times like these that Mildred yearned for the old fashioned phones with the receivers one could slam down with satisfying finality. *Not that I'd ever hang up on my mother.* She forced a smile on her face. She'd always been taught the caller can hear your smile ... or scowl. "Yes, Mother. Of course I'll come."

"Excellent. Shall I arrange a date for you?"

Okay, maybe I would hang up on her. "No, I'll bring my own date, thank you."

"Oh! You have someone, then?"

"I'm at work, Mother. I have to go."

"Okay, I'll email you the details. Love you, darling."

She hung up and saw a parking space open up. *My luck is changing!*

Once in the hospital, she stopped by the kiosk and got her liquid salvation ... and a muffin. She took the two items to her office. She'd barely sat before a knock interrupted her. After sipping the coffee, she waved Nia in. "Can I help you?"

"I was wondering if you ever spoke with Tory. She's still acting the same way. I asked her to swap days with me for Friday, and she got really snotty."

Mildred rubbed her face, wondering where that change in luck had gone. "So, you wanted Friday instead of Saturday?"

"No, I'm already working Friday."

Mildred was pretty sure of the answer, but she checked the schedule to make sure. "So is Tory."

Nia's mouth dropped open. Then she closed and opened it like a fish out of water. She finally narrowed her eyes. "Why didn't Tory tell me? You can ask Dwight, he was there. Tory just said 'no' and never told me why."

"Okay, I'll do that. As for following up with your last complaint, I made several observations over the last two months. I was going to schedule a meeting with you in a week or two, so you coming in was good. You need to fix your work ethic if you want to continue to work here. I've asked Dennis to keep an eye on your improvement. You spread rumors about other people in the department, you gossip, and you avoid patients you don't like. I would like for you to spend your time focusing more on the job, and less on the other people you work with."

As Mildred spoke, Nia's face scrunched up with anger, but she didn't speak. When Mildred finished, Nia nodded with a blank face. "Is that all?"

"For now, yes."

Nia shifted to sit ramrod straight. She spoke with a tight voice. "Thank you for your observations. I need to finish my shift. If there's nothing else, then I'll see you the next time you're in the ER."

Mildred nodded. "Sounds good."

Once Nia was gone, Mildred sent a quick email to Dennis letting him know she'd had her meeting with Nia. She cc'd Andy so he'd know as well.

She checked her schedule and saw she had a two-hour meeting scheduled starting in ten minutes. She had another meeting later that afternoon. There was a conference call in between. It was only half past eight, and already she wanted to lay her head on her desk and escape!

Is it too late to call in sick?

By the end of the day, Mildred stumbled to her car. Between paperwork and meetings, she missed the days of working with patients. She decided to go to the bar near her house. She never did that, but after starting the day with her mother's phone call, and following up with everything that happened, she needed a drink.

After parking at her apartment to change into jeans, a T-shirt, and tennis shoes, she walked the short distance to Seven Stars Brewing Company. The establishment had a U-shaped bar to the right of the door and a juke box along the wall. Across from the door was an electronic dart board, and an old fashioned one was on the far wall, near a back door that led to a patio. There were a few tables scattered around the room to the left of the door and a few tables outside. The place was known for making excellent food.

Mildred walked up to one of the available stools along the bar. "I'll have a whiskey sour and a plate of onion rings."

Her drink came first, and Mildred drank it quickly and ordered a second. She was sipping her third, and the room was starting to tilt, when the onion rings came. She knew she should stop and go home, but she needed to wait until things stopped spinning.

How am I going to find a date? Fuck! But I can't let Mother set me up anymore. I'm done with that.

"What kind of date are you looking for?"

Mildred hadn't meant to say the words out loud. She almost fell from the seat as she spun to see who'd asked her the question.

Chapter 13 - Out for a Six-Pack
Tory

Tory lay on one of the living room couches, watching TV. The house was relatively quiet. Orin worked from home, but almost everyone else was at work or attended school, and then after-school care, and would be out for a bit longer. Tory wasn't on the schedule until later in the week. She usually worked the full weekend, but she had Saturday off this week, which was exciting. Maybe she would find a date for once. She laughed at herself. She hadn't dated since college. *Who has the time ... except maybe Dwight!*

As the blue box on the screen disappeared from the alien planet and the eerie music began to play, she turned off the television. She didn't have many afternoons alone for her shows, but she did have a few guilty pleasures she carved time for.

The back door to the garage clicked open, and she heard Rainy, the six-year-old, bound in, full of energy, despite a full day of school activities. *Oh, to be young.*

Jolly walked in and smiled at her. "Anyone else home, yet?"

"Nope, you're the first, but Tamsin should be here soon. Her classes are done, aren't they?"

The back door opened again, and Maria's voice floated in ahead of her and Georgette appearing. "And then the customer asked that I set up a training to teach his new staff how to work the email."

Georgette chuckled. "The email? Really? I thought by this time everyone knew how to use email, at least. And isn't that a bit below our pay-grade?"

"Right? I'll pass this up the line first thing tomorrow. If I have to go onsite to train people on proper etiquette in emails and the do's and don't's of the email system, I may just come down with a major illness."

Tory snorted to herself as she listened in on the story.

The two walked into the living room. Maria spotted Tory. "You'll help me come up with something that will keep me out of the office for a few weeks, right? Just long enough for my current nightmare of a client to go away?"

Tory sat up and smiled wide. "I'm sure we could come up with something."

Georgette sat down next to Tory. "So, you're home for the night?"

"I am. Dinner and the evening after. I'm thinking of an exciting night of maybe reading."

Maria stopped on the way to a couch. "Why don't we go to the Seven Stars? We haven't been there in forever!"

Jolly sighed. "Do you think Joyce would watch Rainy? I'd love a night out."

Tamsin came in from the back. "What trouble are you getting into?"

Spinning to face her, Maria shimmied. "The Seven Stars. Tonight."

The alpha looked pained. "I promised Paige I'd take her out tonight. But all of you should go."

In the end, they collected six packmates to descend on the bar. Besides Tory, Georgette, Maria, and Jolly, Blake and Orin decided to join them.

After dinner, Tory headed up to her room. She'd been lazing about in leggings and a sweatshirt. Though comfy, they weren't bar clothes. It had been awhile since she wore anything but scrubs or relaxed wear. For several minutes, she just gaped at her clothes, unsure what would work. With a shake, she broke out of her stupor and started filing through the clothes. When she got to the back of her closet, she discovered some dresses and skirts.

She grabbed a pleated black mini skirt. Searching her dresser, she found a sky-blue silk tank top and fishnet stockings. After slipping into flats, she met the others by the front door. The bar was a few blocks away. A nice walk.

When they got there, it was crowded, but Georgette performed her magic, and found them a small table they could crowd around. Maria and Blake headed to the bar and ordered a pitcher of margarita. Tory let the sound of the people talking and the beat of the loud music fill her. It'd been so long since she'd been out at night, her body wanted to soak it all in.

She started to sway with the music, eyes closed, listening to her friends talk. Eventually, she heard the clinking of pitcher and glasses against the wood, and she forced herself back to the present. The cool drink tasted sweet, and the chill refreshed her.

After downing the first glass, Tory finally looked around the bar. A couple played darts; they weren't bad. She could barely see the bar through the crowd. The tables were filled. A few were covered with the smell of the greasy goodness of food from the kitchen. She leaned in. "I'm going to order some onion rings and mozzarella sticks."

Blake's eyes widened. "They have those here? For real? I didn't know they served food."

Tory laughed. "Does anyone want anything else?"

Jolly lifted her glass. "Another round."

"Sounds good."

The path wasn't straight. It was good she was small and well-versed in weaving her way through tight spaces. When she got to the bar, she found a small opening to squeeze in. It took her a few minutes to catch the attention of one of the bartenders. When one approached, she put in her order.

"Give me ten, love, and I'll have it all ready." She took Tory's credit card, swiped it, then handed it back. She was off to another customer faster than Tory could put the card away.

Next to her, a woman mumbled. If she weren't a werewolf, with super hearing, she wouldn't have heard a thing. "How am ... find a date? Fuck! Can't let Mother set me up 'more. Done with that."

Tory turned to see Mildred, her boss, sitting there, at least two sheets to the wind. Amusement warred with concern. She'd never seen the woman anything but put-together. "What kind of date are you looking for?"

She wasn't sure why she asked. It wasn't like she could help Mildred out; she was Tory's boss. But she sounded miserable.

Mildred's head snapped to Tory, her eyes working to focus. Despite the struggle, Tory was momentarily struck by how pretty her eyes were. "Tory, wha are you doin' here?"

Tory smiled. "I'm here with some friends. How about you?"

"Jus' a quick drin'." She waved her empty glass. "Oh! Is gone. I should get more."

"No, I don't think you should. Do you need a ride home?"

The other woman shook her head as if trying to clear it. "Am I goin' home now?"

Tory squeezed her eyes shut, then took a deep breath before opening her eyes to wave down a bartender. "Two waters, please." She turned back to her boss. "After a bit of water." Once Mildred had drunk half her water, Tory tried again. "So, tell me why you need a date. What is this about your mother?"

Mildred rubbed her face. "Not 'portant. Gallery Saturday. I find someone."

Tory took a sip of water. *I have the night off, and I would like visiting a gallery, but would this be crossing some sort of line? It doesn't sound like she actually wants a date, just someone along to placate her parents. I mean ... maybe I could help.*

"I could go with you, I mean, if you want. I understand it isn't really a date. But, you could tell your parents, get them off your back."

"But you're girl."

A laugh burst from Tory, interrupting the people on her other side. "Well, yes, I've noticed. If that's a problem, then I wish you nothing but luck." *Well, maybe no line will be crossed ... if this is happening. Too bad ... or not, it isn't like I'd date my boss.* Tory shook her head at the conflicting thoughts.

"No, I like girls, parents don't know. Big fight."

Tory's mind momentarily stuttered, uncertain how to take the information. Was a date a possibility? *No! She's still your boss. You're just offering to help her out. Gah!*

"Ah. Got it. Well, as I see it, you have to tell them eventually. With me there, it could be with someone you don't have to worry about losing. But I don't have any urge to push you out of the closet if you like the safety of where you are."

It was Mildred's turn to shut her eyes. After a minute, Tory's order arrived. She was about to walk away when Mildred opened her eyes. "Yes. Please. Saturday. Thank you."

Chapter 14 - Survey Says, You Can't React at an Event
Mildred

For the ten millionth time, Mildred wondered what she was doing bringing Tory to her aunt's gallery event. She'd debated with herself over and over the merits of a date—even a fake date—with a work underling. The problem was, she only had Tory's number from her work file, and calling or texting that way seemed wrong. She could approach the other woman in person, but that would be at work and inappropriate.

In the end, Mildred decided to go ahead with the plans they'd devised that night in the bar. She'd pick Tory up at six at The Zesty Bean. Tory had suggested the coffee shop because it was near the bar and where she lived. Mildred realized that if it was close to where Tory lived, then the two of them didn't live far apart.

One more thing she tried not to think about.

This isn't a real date. Tory is doing me a favor; she isn't really interested.

A gallery event meant Mildred could dress less conservatively. She found a wine-colored dress that clasped below her chest with a circular buckle. It flitted down, barely touching her body in a cool silk waterfall to mid-thigh.

After a final circuit around her apartment to get phone, keys, and purse, she headed out, swallowing her apprehension. *I will have fun tonight. Fuck it.*

Tory stood outside the café in a black cocktail dress and flats. The dress had a few embedded sparkles at the top, highlighting her chest. It was a simple design, but looked good on her ... really good. It took Mildred a moment to realize she held two to-go cups from the café.

After pulling up in front of her, Tory placed one cup on top of the car long enough to open the door, then handed the other to Mildred. "I didn't want to be a tease, drinking coffee in front of you without offering you one. It has a splash of milk and sugar. The other is black. I wasn't sure what you wanted, and we never exchanged numbers." She smiled sheepishly. "I can run in and doctor the other one."

Mildred smiled. "Sounds perfect. Though, I'll drink black as well."

"No, take that one, I'll go quickly add some milk and sugar to this one. Give me a minute. You can stay here; it's an actual legal spot to park. Shocking, I know."

Before Mildred could argue, the wicked fast woman was in and out and back to the car. She buckled herself in and sipped her coffee. "I love their coffee. I have a friend whose coffee is better, but Zesty Bean's is excellent."

"I'm intrigued. Better than this? I'd love to try it."

Tory leaned back, resting her head on the seat. "I don't know. Maybe one day."

They drove in silence for a few minutes while Mildred navigated weekend traffic. Tory hummed a bit, enjoying her coffee. It surprised Mildred how much the sounds intrigued her.

She cleared her throat. "Maybe we should talk about what to expect when we get to the gallery."

Straightening, Tory smiled at her. "Sounds good. Is it more than walking around, enjoying art?"

"Yeah." Mildred sighed. *How can I explain this and not sound crazy? Well, I guess I crossed the line of crazy when I had to appease my parents as an adult.* "The short story is, my parents want me married with kids."

One of Tory's eyebrows shot up, slipping behind her blue bangs. "You do know—*they* will know—that that won't be possible with me, right? Not without adoption or something exterior."

A laugh bubbled out of Mildred. "Yeah, that. They don't know I like women. I've never told them. They keep setting me up with random men, each one worse than the last."

"So, what? I'm going to be a surprise? Are we going to cause a scene?" Tory's voice stayed calm as she spoke, but Mildred knew the other woman must be getting irritated. She'd be frustrated ... she *was* frustrated.

"Yes. I mean, I didn't mean to put you in this position. I kept trying to figure out how to cancel this week. I didn't think doing it at work would be appropriate, and, as you said, we didn't exchange numbers."

Tory made a sound deep in her throat. "If I wasn't with you, this game you're playing with your parents would continue?"

"Yes."

"And you hate it?"

"Yes. Wait, I didn't say that."

She snorted. "Your voice and story said it clearly enough."

Mildred's face scrunched up. *Do I hate it? I know I don't like it, but hate?* She drove for a bit, thinking about her emotions and feelings at her parents'—her mother's—ministrations. "I guess ... you know, I think ... yeah, I really get to the point I don't want to be around my family when I know they're going to throw random men at me. And I love them, even when they want to pair me up with awful people. In the end, they do want the best for me."

Tory chuckled. "Family always does. Trust me, I have a lot of family. I understand how that works."

"So, you aren't mad at me about this? I figured you were about to ask me to take you back."

Tory gazed down at herself. "Look, I put on a pretty dress, I have the night off, I haven't been out on a date, fake or not, in ... well, I don't know the last time I went out. I don't really care about the drama. I just want to see pretty pictures, have fancy wine given to me, and if I'm really lucky, food."

Relief washed through Mildred. "There will definitely be food, and the food will be excellent."

"So, what do we tell your parents? Is this our first date? Second?"

Mildred slouched, grumbling. "That's an excellent question. I think the best thing to do is try not to veer too far from the truth. How about this is our second date?"

"Makes sense. We ran into each other at a bar, and realized we got along great?"

"Maybe not that. When you meet my family, you'll see why they wouldn't love that we met at a bar. Maybe we ran into each other at the Zesty Bean before work. We realized we had common interests and it led to this."

Tory nodded as Mildred babbled on. "Okay, coffee shop. Will your family ask? How many details do we need?"

With a sigh, Mildred realized she was right. "Probably not that many. You're right, their biggest issue will be me showing up with a woman, not a man. The questions may not get past that." Mildred took a deep breath, trying to focus her scattered thoughts. "Okay, we're almost there. We can do this."

"Who are you trying to convince?"

Mildred pulled into a spot and turned off the car. She continued to hold the steering wheel, bracing herself for the next few hours of her day.

Tory unbuckled and turned to her. "Ready?"

"No, but let's do this anyway."

Mildred finished the last of her coffee and got out of her car. As they approached the door, her heart pounded faster and faster. *Please, don't let this ruin my aunt's event. I just want my parents to stop.*

She pulled open the door and a wave of cold air hit her, sending a wash of chills down her back. Behind her, Tory huffed. "Whoa, I should've bought a sweater. It's cold in there. Take me to the wine."

"Sounds good to me." Mildred took Tory's hand and placed it on her arm, so they'd approach her family together.

The gallery had three rooms of art. Each room was filled with beautiful people milling around in small groups, drinking, eating, and discussing the art.

A server in black slacks, a stiff white button down, and a black tie held out a tray with bacon wrapped scallops. Next to her Tory groaned. "Can we take two?"

"Sure, but there'll be plenty. Don't fill up too quickly."

"Oh, I won't."

A few steps farther, and another server offered them wine.

As they made their way through the first room, Tory split her focus between the art on the walls and the food being waved in their faces. Mildred just wanted to find her parents.

When they got to the second room, she found them.

"Mildred, darling, you made it! Come, introduce us to your date!"

This is it. She tried to breathe but suddenly forgot how.

"Relax, Mildred. What's the worst that can happen? They won't make a scene, will they? It's your aunt's event. Relax."

Mildred realized how tense she was and tried to release some of the tension she held. Her mother reached her. "Oh! You didn't bring a date, you brought a friend." And all her muscles tightened back up.

There was a moment of silence while Mildred debated what she wanted to do. Then she shook her head. "No, not just a friend, mother. Date. I told you I was bringing a date, and that's what I've done."

Tory slid her hand from Mildred's arm and wrapped it around her waist. She held her other hand out. "Hi, my name's Tory."

Mildred's mother held herself still, like a statue. A small smile plastered on her face. "You brought Tory as your date?" Her head tilted ever so slightly, and her smile widened. "It is a pleasure to meet you. My name is Priscilla Quincy. You may call me Priscilla. My husband will be thrilled to meet the woman who finally captured our daughter's heart. Come, you must meet everyone."

Her mother maneuvered Tory until she had the shorter woman under her arm and led her away.

Mildred stood, dumbfounded. *What just happened?*

Chapter 15 - Then it's a Date
Tory

The gallery was fantastic. All the art amazed Tory. If she could afford it, she'd buy something for her room in the pack house. The problem, this was an event for "who's who" in Santa Cruz and everything was out of her budget.

She'd heard about these events, but she never thought she'd attend one.

She was glad Blake had a dress she could borrow. She didn't own anything fancy enough for something like this.

When Priscilla, Mildred's mother, collected Tory to meet Mildred's father, she could feel—practically taste—Mildred's nervousness, but there wasn't much she could do without causing a ruckus.

"Albert. Albert, honey. Come meet Tory."

"Is that the man Mildred brought?" Priscilla led Tory to an older man with thinning dark hair and sharp blue eyes that Tory sensed didn't miss a thing. He was a bit thick around the middle, but his suit was expertly tailored. He had a mustache but was otherwise clean-shaven.

"No, dear. Tory is a woman."

The man laughed. "I told you years ago you had it wrong. If you'd listened to me, you could've been finding her matches that may have ended in marriage years ago." His eyes narrowed as he took in Tory with her black and blue dyed hair and borrowed dress. "No offense to you, Tory, if you and my daughter have found love. It's just, she never told us. A few of our friends have lesbian daughters we could have introduced Mildred to if we'd only known."

Mildred finally caught up to them. "How about you let *me* worry about who I date, Father, and you worry about your life and your business."

He turned to her, his face, the model of impassivity. "Of course, Mildred. I just wish you'd told us you liked women. I don't know why you decided to tell us this way."

Tory snatched a salmon pâté on a cracker from a passing server.

"It's not something I'm trying to 'do' to you, I just wasn't sure how to tell you. I know Tory loves art. When I mentioned this, she asked to come.

That isn't even that much of a lie. I do love art, and I did offer to come tonight. Another server walked by with wine, and Tory switched out both hers and Mildred's.

Pricilla placed a hand on her husband's arm. "It's fine, love. Let's just enjoy the evening and the fact that Mildred is sharing this part of her life."

Albert's mouth tightened before he nodded. "You're right, dear, as always. I apologize, Tory, you didn't need to be dragged into all of this. Please, enjoy the art, the food, and the drinks. This should be a night to relax and savor."

She and Mildred were about to step away when her mother cleared her throat. "One more thing."

Mildred sighed. "Yes, Mother."

"I'd really like to get to know you, Tory. Why don't the two of you come for dinner Friday night?"

Tory shook her head. "I'm sorry, I work Friday night. I tend to work weekends, and most nights."

Her mom's brow furrowed. "Is there a night you don't work?"

Tory dug in her purse for her phone. It took a few minutes to get to the schedule, but once she found it, she said, "I don't work Thursday night this week."

Mildred's mother's face lit up. "Perfect. We'll see the two of you at the house for dinner. You aren't a vegetarian?"

Albert scoffed. "We saw her eating the salmon hors d'oeuvres."

Priscilla's mouth tightened before she smiled wide. "Any other dietary restrictions?"

"No," Tory said. "I'll eat just about anything."

As she and Mildred toured the art, she leaned in. "Did I agree to dinner on Thursday?"

"My mother is very good."

Tory downed a glass of wine, then started coughing. "That wasn't wine." She looked at the glass and noticed it was a different color. "Some of these have harder liquor in them."

Mildred took the glass from her and guided her to a side table with glasses of what she hoped was water. "My aunt likes wine and vodka cranberry. You can usually tell the difference by the types of glasses. They're served in similar glasses, but the wine glasses are wider. They also have colored stems."

"Is there a guide?"

"Probably by the door. We came in too quickly. I should've let you look at the literature. Are you okay?"

Tory shut her eyes for a moment and took stock. "Yeah, I'm fine. It was just a bit of a shock." She licked her lips, then laughed at how ridiculous everything was. "How are you?"

"I'm good. Are you okay with continuing this farce? You don't have to."

"It's fine. I don't have anything else on my dance card. That's a thing, right, a dance card?"

Mildred laughed, and Tory enjoyed the sound. "It is. When I was young I even had one or two."

Tory snorted. "That's amazing."

They spent the rest of the evening enjoying the gallery. Tory showed Mildred her favorite paintings, and Mildred explained the inspiration behind them. They both loved some of the paintings of people and still-lifes, but a forest scene with a wolf stole Tory's heart.

Sunday was a full moon. Tory woke up early and went into work during the day. It didn't happen often, but she did work a few days. She returned to pack house by dinner.

Paige sat in the living room. "I can't believe you made it back by dinner!"

"Connie's cooking. Why wouldn't I be here?"

Georgette walked in from the kitchen carrying a steaming mug of coffee. The aroma saturated Tory's tired body. "Because you knew we'd grill you about last night and your date with the cutie."

"Shower first, then maybe." Tory reached for the mug Georgette held out to her.

"Coffee first. Otherwise, you'll drown before you get clean, and I want details."

Tory laughed and she trudged up the stairs. "Why don't you just find someone to date yourself?"

"I don't want to date. I just want to hear stories. Now, hurry up!"

After her shower, Tory put on loose shorts and a tank top. Dinner was right before their run and putting on anything fancier would be a waste.

The new wolf, Jett, Tamsin's student, was at dinner. Tory had met her with the pack the previous weekend, and was happy she'd decided to run with them. Not to mention, with her here, no one was interrogating Tory about her evening with Mildred.

Tory let her mind wander, imagining herself sitting on a couch drinking wine with Mildred, enjoying the artwork they'd seen the night before. She blinked, bringing herself back to the discussion with Jett, hoping to help her feel comfortable with the pack.

Once they got outside, Tamsin started them shifting in waves. Tory was in the first wave. She quickly stripped and let her wolf out. The pain of her body morphing, bones reshaping, hair receding and growing in new places, always took her breath away. Pain.

But then her black beauty was out and ready to play. She took off with Orin, Connie, and Georgette. They ran down the path. *Is that a new family of cats in our backyard? I need to come out and run more, scare those silly beasts off! And a pair of dogs? Oh, they love the cats. And a family of squirrels.*

The scents of the trail slowed her to a walk as she imagined a story with each of the different creatures that lived near their home. Georgette snorted, signaling to Tory to hurry up.

She ran.

They arrived at the meeting spot and waited. It didn't take long for the rest of the pack to join them.

Tamsin led them away. Tory let her mind unfocus as her body stretched, legs pumped, and fur blew in the wind.

Am I really going through with this pretending to date Mildred? What am I hoping to get out of it? She's nice ... pretty ... smart. But she's not really interested in me, is she? Well, at least I can get out of the house, and my routine, for a few days. Thursday will probably be the end of it.

She got knocked out of her thoughts as Tamsin called them into a hunt. Lifting her snout, Tory caught the scent of a deer. Joyfully, she howled as she followed her pack, her family, for their monthly celebration of the moon.

Chapter 16 - Nothing to See Here, Businesses as Usual
Mildred

Monday morning, Mildred weaved her way through the people heading home after a full moon weekend. They looked tired and worn out. She met Andy by the coffee kiosk. "Anything I need to know about?"

"Much of the same. We had two patients diagnosed with heart attacks. The pattern Tory discovered of pulmonary embolisms have become heart attacks. Beyond that, nothing out of the ordinary. Next month is when the real fun begins."

"Tory what now?"

"You haven't heard? Dennis hasn't come to report it to you?"

Andy and Mildred had made it to her office, and she plopped into her chair behind a mountain of papers. She spent a few moments with her coffee before she yawned wide. "Okay, again, Tory what now?"

Andy laughed. "You should ask her when she gets in tonight."

Mildred scowled and Andy threw up his hands. "I'm not saying I won't tell you now. I see you're not willing to wait, though, you should follow up with the young nurse. She has the details you'll want."

"Promise. Now talk."

He explained that over two months seven homeless patients had come in with their oddly consistent diagnosis. Recently, the pulmonary embolisms diagnosis had shifted to heart attacks.

"That's odd, but that doesn't mean anything, does it?"

"Tory believes it does."

Mildred leaned back. "I think I need more coffee. I'll talk with her when she comes in and get this all figured out. It sounds like a run of bad luck. Anything else?"

"Not here. How was the gallery?"

"My aunt's work was amazing, as always."

Andy smiled. "I'm sure it was. And did your parents arrange for a horrible date?"

The blush heated Mildred's neck and cheeks.

Andy's eyes widened. "Do not tell me they finally found someone you like?"

"No, it isn't that. I ... they ... um." She picked up her coffee and took a sip.

"I've never seen you so flustered. For God's sake, woman. Talk." He leaned forward, his elbows on her desk.

She carefully put the cup on the one clear spot, away from papers and her calendar, which informed her she had three meetings before two that afternoon. Some of the levity of the situation died at the reminder of all her work. She sighed. "I brought Tory with me. She—"

"Tory?" Andy gasped. "Our Tory? Or did you find another one out and about town?"

"If you'd let me finish. I was out at a bar last week after work, and I ran into her. She agreed to be my plus one at the event."

"My goodness. How did Priscilla and Albert take it?"

"They want us to come over for dinner on Thursday so they can properly get to know her."

Andy's jaw hit the table. "Wait, do they think the two of you are an item? *Are* the two of you an item? Do you like our blue-haired vixen? I'm not saying I disapprove; I'm just amazed you would date. You're such a lone wolf."

Mildred threw a pencil at her friend. She felt her cheeks blaze hotter. *Why am I blushing? Tory and I are just work colleagues. We don't have romantic feelings for each other. This isn't anything embarrassing.*

"No, we're not an item. This is just to give me a breather from the pestering ways of my family. Tory agreed to play the part of my girlfriend, that's it."

"And she agreed? She met your parents, and she agreed?"

"I know. It seems highly unlikely, but yeah. The meeting was short." Mildred shook her head. "Thursday won't be."

Andy laughed. "No, it won't be. And I can't wait until Friday to get the scoop."

By three, Mildred was ready to scream or fall over dead. She hated days that were full of meetings. It made her miss working full time with patients. *Why did I want to move up to administration?*

She decided she needed a pick-me-up and visited the coffee kiosk for her favorite brew. She saw Tory heading in as she paid.

"Tory, do you have a minute?"

"I need to go check in and see if Dennis needs me right away, but after that I could zip up to your office."

"Good, I heard about your homeless person project. If you have any reports, bring them along."

Her face froze, and she nodded.

Mildred returned to her office and plowed through the piles of paperwork. Eventually, a knock came to her door. She looked up to see Tory. A warmth bloomed in her before she remembered she was at work. She shook it off. "Come in, take a seat."

Mildred filled her in on why she'd requested her presence.

Tory grimaced. "I'm sorry if I should've brought you my thoughts on this earlier. I spoke to some of the other nurses, and they said I was being silly, and I shouldn't bother you."

It didn't escape Mildred that Tory didn't name anyone specific. It frustrated her as a boss, but warmed her as a friend that she was so loyal. In the end, she decided it wasn't important enough to learn the names of the other people who knew; the matter was small.

"Just so you know, I don't think any issue is too minor to be brought to my attention. Andy filled me in on the basics, but I'd like to see what you've found."

Tory nodded, then showed Mildred the data she'd collected, starting back in July, on homeless people brought into the emergency room. Though it was odd to have so many with first pulmonary embolisms and then heart attacks, Mildred wasn't sure it was anything worth reporting to anyone higher up. "Why are you so concerned about all of this?"

Tory bit her lip. "I just can't believe this is random—that there would be this many people within a community having these issues."

"But, Tory, what else could it be? It isn't like you can give another person a pulmonary embolism, punch someone on the shoulder and give them a heart attack. You know it doesn't work that way. These are personal diagnoses not infectious diseases."

"I know, it's just ... odd. I don't like this kind of odd. I think we should keep track, and since I'm the only one who's worried, I'll do the bookwork."

Mildred shrugged. "As you wish."

Chapter 17 - Get Your Story Straight - Ma'am Tory

"Get up, lazy!" Georgette flopped on the couch next to Tory, lifting Tory's legs and dropping her feet onto her lap. "I'm guessing you collapsed here when you got home, but aren't you getting picked up soon?"

Adrenaline shot through Tory almost as fast as she leapt to her feet. "Holy hell, what time is it? Is Blake home? I need something to wear, and a shower, gods above, and coffee!"

Flying off the couch, she ran up the stairs to the sound of Georgette's laughter. The other woman yelled after her, "I'll get you some coffee and find Blake while you clean up. You have a few minutes, friend, slow down and breathe!"

Once showered, Tory padded into her room, a plush towel wrapped around her body. She found a steaming cup of coffee on her dresser. Lying on her bed was a light purple sleeveless dress. The skirt fanned out like a reversed umbrella. "Thank you Blake," she yelled.

Blake's voice came back, soft with distance. "Don't forget nylons. You're being fancy."

Tory snorted. *Me, fancy. That's a hoot.*

Fitted to her waist with a lace back, the dress didn't work with a bra, but that was fine. The pleated skirt ended just above her knees. She found black nylons in the back of her dresser. *When the hell did I get these? I may need to go shopping if Mildred and I continue this farce.*

She slipped on her black flats, grabbed the small purse she'd used at the gallery event, and slid her wallet and phone into it. With a sigh, she gave her reflection a quick look. *As good as it gets. Why am I so worried? This isn't a real date. What does it matter if anyone doesn't approve? If they all think I'm awful, there's reason to say this is our last date.*

She let out a huff of air, ruffling her bangs.

Tory left her room and headed down to the living room. Making a detour to the kitchen, she debated another cup of coffee, but decided she'd had all the liquid magic she should before the night began. *Do they serve coffee at fancy dinners? What have I gotten myself into?*

Back in the living room, she found Blake, Georgette, and Paige. Paige smiled at her. "You look great. Have fun on your fake date."

She smiled and rolled her eyes. "I know, this is all silly."

Georgette shrugged. "I'm just happy you're getting out of the house and having fun."

"I agree!" Blake said. "Just let me know how many of my fancy dresses you need. I may be a foot taller than you, but we seem to wear the same size dresses, and on you, they're appropriate."

A smile spread across her face as she looked down at the dress. "I'm not that short!"

The others laughed. Georgette shook her head. "At least half a foot, sweety. Are you even five feet tall?"

"Five two. Maybe even taller. I should learn to walk in heels."

Still chuckling, Paige asked, "And how tall is this mystery woman?"

A bark of laughter burst from Blake. "If I remember correctly, taller than me."

Heading to the door, Tory shook her head. "I hate you all."

"No, you don't!" Georgette's voice followed her. "You love us. Now stay safe and have a good time. Remember, I'll want to hear about all that lovely food."

"Whatever." She grumbled as she shut the door behind her, cutting off the amused chatter. Once it was closed, she laughed at her pack mates' antics.

She walked to The Zesty Bean. Mildred was already there waiting for her. She slipped into the front seat. "Sorry I'm late. I fell asleep after work."

Mildred laughed. "No worries. I can't imagine how messed up your sleep schedule is."

"Eh." Tory shrugged as Mildred pulled away from the curb. "I'm used to sleeping when and wherever I can."

They drove in silence for a few minutes before Tory's stress about the evening overcame her. "I'm not sure how you think this is going to go, but if we're going to put a show on for your parents, should we have some details down about our dating history and each other?"

Mildred tensed and came to a sharp stop at the red light. *Crap! Maybe I shouldn't have brought that up so abruptly.*

She took a slow breath and nodded. "You're right. And I'm sorry. None of this is fair of me to ask of you."

Tory chuckled. "It's fine. You seem to be in a tight spot. Okay, what do you want to know about me?"

"Tell me about your schooling."

Thinking back on her past, Tory smiled. "I went to high school here in town, then I moved up to San Francisco for my nursing degree. After I graduated, I ended up working there for two years. Then I got a job down in Texas. I didn't love living down there. I missed my friends and family. As soon as I could, I found a way to move back here.

When I got the job at the emergency room, I was over the moon."

"Until you learned who you had to work for?" Mildred joked.

Tory snorted. "Exactly. Dennis is a bear of a man."

Mildred smiled at her. "I went to school in San Francisco as well. UC San Fran?"

"That's the one. But I'm only twenty-seven. I'm guessing you're a year or two older than me?"

Mildred nodded. "Thirty-two."

"Whoa! A whole different decade? I don't know about this any more, Mildred. I mean, fake dating is one thing, but you're in your thirties?"

"I guess I can get out my cane now that the secret's out."

They both laughed, and an excitement for the night and spending more time with Mildred washed through Tory. Kibitzing with her was fun. She watched as the scenery changed from the city, with homes tight together, to an area where homes had more space between them. Everything felt more luxurious. *What am I doing here, I really won't fit in.* She played with the clasp on her purse.

Mildred pulled into a wide driveway with a gate that had a keypad entry. She rolled down her window and quickly typed something in. Tory looked away to avoid any questions that she tried to see the code. Once on Mildred's parent's property, the driveway snaked through trees and curved around a pond until they reached a palatial home. Tory's stomach dropped.

Mildred pulled up to the door and shut off her car. "If you want to leave at any point, just let me know. Again, thank you."

"No worries. If nothing else, I'll get a good meal out of this." She laughed, a bit high-pitched. Her eyes widened. "I will get a good meal out of this, right?"

Mildred opened the door and laughed. "Yes, the food should be excellent. Come on."

The doors opened up to a huge hexagonal foyer. The floor was covered in a white tile, and a chandelier dripping with crystals hung from the ceiling. Staircases led up to the next level on both the left and right side of the entrance. Beneath the stairs were alcoves with tables and large bouquets of flowers. Straight ahead was an archway leading to what looked like a dining room. There were rooms to the left and right as well. So many rooms.

Mildred slipped her arm in Tory's. "This way."

"How do you not get lost?"

"Who said I didn't?"

Tory relaxed as she laughed.

They went through the opening to the left. The living room ... sitting room? Solarium? "What room is this? How many rooms are there in this ... house?"

"This is the drawing room. We'll wait here for my parents. If we'd gone the other way we'd have found the sun room. It's a pretty room during the day when the sun's up, but it's getting late."

"Sun room, like solarium? Your house has a solarium?" Tory waggled her eyebrows at Mildred.

"Yes, exactly."

They sat on one of the smaller couches. A server came over and handed them a glass with something alcoholic-smelling and a small plate with finger foods.

Tory gazed at Mildred with her brows up.

Mildred sniffed the glass. "Wine, merlot. And we have smoked trout croquettes, stuffed mushrooms, goat-cheese-and salami-stuffed dates, and figs-in-a-blanket with goat cheese."

Everything looked amazing. Tory took a sip of the wine. She didn't know a lot about merlot, but it tasted expensive, good, smooth, delicious. Each of the foods on the plate melted in her mouth. Before she could put the plate down, a new one appeared, with each of the offerings. The server asked, "Is everything to your liking, ma'am?"

"Um." Tory looked around the room, trying to figure out what to say. "Yes, it's delicious. Thank you."

Mildred put her hand on Tory's arm. "Do you like all the hors d'oeuvres?"

"Oh! Yes, they're all amazing. I could eat a platter of each of them."

"Oh, no, Tory! Then what would you eat for dinner?" Priscilla, Mildred's mom, walked in from the other side. "We have a full dinner; we don't want you to fill up too soon."

Behind her, Albert, Mildred's dad, came in, a small wide glass filled with an amber liquid in his hand. The two sat on a couch opposite them. "I'm so glad you two made it," Priscilla continued. "Tory, how was your week?"

A moment of panic froze her tongue as everyone turned to her. She licked her lips, then took a sip of the exquisite wine. "It was good. A bit insane but working in the emergency room will always be that way."

Albert sipped his drink and leaned forward. "Oh? How so?"

She shrugged. "You can't plan out your schedule. At any moment you can face, well, anything. Any type of medical issue can come through the door. Any age, any number of people, any situation. We had a car full of high school students flip over last summer."

"Oh, no!" Priscilla said, her hand flying to her chest. "Did they survive?"

Tory mentally kicked herself. She realized she'd started to babble. "Some of them did. They hadn't been wearing their seat belts. But that's just it; you can't prepare for a night like that until the call comes in. On another night we save everyone. But when I walk through the doors, I have no idea which patients I'll see. If I were in a regular clinic, I'd have a schedule, probably set months in advance, but my job is chaos."

Albert tilted his drink towards her. "You sound like you like it."

"I don't know if 'like' is the right word. It suits me. I'm good at what I do."

Mildred rubbed her back. "She really is. When we hired Tory, she came with a great letter of recommendation, but everyone does. Her stills have proven she was the right person to hire. She's good at diagnosis, and also has a lot of patience, as well as being very caring. I've seen her calm the scared, convince the belligerent to listen, and teach the new staff procedures."

Tory had to clamp her mouth shut to stop the shock from showing on her face. *When did*

Mildred see all that? I thought I worked under the radar ... how I like it. I did what I did to help others, not for recognition.

Across from them, Priscilla beamed. "That's excellent. Tory, you sound like the perfect match for our Mildred. She needs someone who will challenge her. She's too smart for her own good, and anyone less so will be kicked to the curb pretty quickly. No wonder you've lasted as long as you have." She gave a sly smile to her husband before shifting it to Mildred. "How long *have* the two of you been an item?"

Mildred opened her mouth, then shut it, quickly glancing at Tory. "Dating someone you work with, who works *for* you is tricky. Tory and I ran into each other at a local coffee house close to both of our homes. We spoke for a bit, and realized we got along. That's how we ended up at the gallery together."

Her mom's eyes practically bulged out of her face. "So, this is your second date?"

Damn it ... the plan! The whole family is too smart for their own good. Why can't any of them be vapid or slow?

Beside her, Mildred sighed. "Technically, yes."

Her mom tittered. "Well, then, we'd better make it a good one!"

Chapter 18 - Mother's Madness
Mildred

Mildred worked to hide the myriad emotions that fought for dominance as her mother tried to figure out her relationship with Tory. Hell, she didn't understand their relationship. Before they went to the gallery, she'd only observed her a few times. When she'd laid out her observations for her parents, she realized she'd spoken the truth.

I guess I've learned more about Tory than I realized. I don't want to waste her time any more than I have. I'll have to tell her on the way back to the city that this is it. It could've been worse; we seem to get along well together. Her gut clenched at the idea of ending things, but she knew it was for the best.

"Mildred, dear, why don't you give Tory a tour of the house and we can meet in the dining room. Dinner should be ready in twenty minutes."

Pulled from her musings, she nodded. "Sounds great, Mother."

She stood and took Tory's hand. "Let's start the way we came, then we can swing back this way."

"So we can see the solarium?" Her eyes twinkled.

"Yes, while there's still a bit of sun to enjoy it."

"Oh!" Mother said. "The solarium is beautiful this time of day. You'll love it. That's the perfect place to start the tour. Very romantic. Go to the conservatory through the library after that, darling."

"Yes, Mother."

"It really is the best place to start," Father added, his eyes twinkling mischievously. She got the feeling he liked Tory. She was flabbergasted again about how wrong all her assumptions about her parents and her dating had been.

Mildred made a quick exit before she was given any more advice. They passed through the foyer to the solarium. Two of the walls and the ceiling were windows inlaid with black wrought iron dividers. Instead of the walls meeting the ceiling at a ninety degree angle, it curved, giving a smooth view of the sky above, which was painted a furious red and orange with the coming of the sunset.

Next to her, Tory sighed. "I would spend every night in here gazing at the beauty of that sky. Wow! Unbelievable." The other woman glided forward, as if floating, towards the windows, until she was only a few inches away, and sighed again. "It's just so pretty."

Like you. Mildred shook herself, not sure where that thought came from. *This is a hoax, not a real relationship.*

"I'm glad you love it." She walked up behind Tory and lifted her hands to place them on the other woman's shoulders. At the last moment she remembered they didn't know each other well enough and made fists, lowering her arms. "I have another area you'll love, before I show you the east wing."

Tory swung around, mirth on her face. "You describe your home as having wings?" Her light blue eyes twinkled.

"Well ..." Heat flooded her face. *Damn blush!* "Yes. Since we have two directions from the foyer, one east and one west, we call them the east wing and the west wing. It's easier."

Tory bit her lips. She looked like she was holding back violent laughter. "You could be more creative. You know, like the sun wing and the boring wing, or business wing. Moon wing. Dragon and phoenix? Anything? Bueller?"

A wide smile almost hurt Mildred's cheeks. "I'll take that under advisement." She reached out and slid her hand into Tory's. "But for now, let's move on to the library."

"A whole library? Your house has a library. You know how insane that sounds, right?"

"Look, if we're going to have a dragon wing, we have to appease the dragons. Sun, books, and food. I don't make the rules, I just have to serve the beasts."

Tory laughed as Mildred led her to the next room. "Fair enough. Never go against the dragons, for they are fierce, and we are tasty."

The library had always been Mildred's sanctuary. The room was floor-to-ceiling books, complete with a sliding ladder. There were large chairs with lamps at both ends of the room, and skylights in the ceiling to allow for natural light during the day.

Tory stopped in the middle of the room, gaping at all the books. "Is there an urban fantasy section? Historical romance? Contemporary romance?"

Mildred clasped Tory's shoulders and rotated her towards the far wall. "All the books along that wall are fiction, as well as that one." She pointed to the wall that backed up to the solarium. "My parents let me read what I liked when I was a kid, and we stored most of the books here. I had two bookcases in my room as well."

"Is your room on this floor, too?"

Mildred shivered, thinking about bringing the spunky woman in her bedroom. "No, the bedrooms are all upstairs." Her voice had dropped and sounded huskier. What was the matter with her? This was all play-acting to appease her mother. She shook her head. "Let's keep moving. Mother will loose the hounds if we're late for the first course."

Tory stopped half-way through her turn. "Courses? How many courses will be in this dinner?"

Slipping her fingers in Tory's, Mildred led her to the conservatory. "Five or six courses. I never know what Mother plans."

The extension to the house was more of a semi-detached room with flowers and plants growing around the edges. There was a bench down the center where they could sit.

"This is beautiful. An indoor garden. Is there an outdoor garden, too?" Tory stepped away to investigate the growing things and smell the flowers.

"There is. Maybe we can go look at it after dinner. There are lights and pathways."

"Excellent. What's next on our tour?"

"You aren't bored?"

Tory shook her head. "This is fantastic. Life of the rich and famous ... or rich, at least."

"I'd love to deny that my family is rich, but that would be a hard sell." She ducked her head with a small laugh. "Okay, I doubt going into the kitchen would be a good idea."

They headed through the library to a hallway that circumnavigated the foyer. They went through the dining room into another corridor. At the far end, they entered a family room. The room was big with an area of couches, desks, a television, and a table for family games.

Tory walked to a big open spot, stretched out her arms and spun. "So much space. It's beautiful." As her skirt flared, Mildred thought Tory was pretty beautiful, too.

She stopped and grinned at Mildred. "How much more house do you have? I can't believe this is where you grew up! Why do you work at the hospital when you have all this?"

"Would you stop being a nurse if you had this?"

The other woman bit her lip, her eyes widening. "No. I wouldn't. I have a desire to help people. No amount of riches would get me to want to stop, even if I won the lottery. Maybe if I had enough money and a reason, I'd want to work less, or more days, less nights, but I can't imagine not wanting to work."

"Then you get it. I've been trying to explain that to my parents."

Some of the light dimmed in Tory. "Do they want you to quit?"

"Maybe not quit but cut back. They've always wanted me to take over the family's banking business. And, of course, they want me to get married. It's a society thing."

"Do they care about you being in love first?"

Mildred's mouth screwed up to the side. "My parents love me. In the end, they want what's best for me, but sometimes they get caught up in what's happening around them."

"So, where does this leave us—you and me? If this is our last date, will they continue to throw people at you? Will they start to pair you up with women now?" Tory sounded composed, but her body was tight as she asked her questions.

"Probably. Father called this week and told me about all his friends with lesbian daughters. I knew about some of them; I just didn't know he did. None of those set-ups will work. If they would've, it would have happened already. That said, don't worry. I won't expect you to participate in this farce after tonight."

Tory's face scrunched up. "I'm more worried about you. All I really do is work and hang out with my family. You're the one who has random dates thrown at you. That would drive me crazy. But if you're pretending to be with me ... do you want to find someone?"

"Not right now. My parents want to marry me off. I just want to focus on my work, and let things happen naturally. I also don't think my dream woman will show up at a society event. If I was going to find her at one, I feel like I would've by now."

Tory smiled. "That makes sense."

They walked back to the hallway in the direction of the den, the next room towards the dining room. "Anyway, I wanted to thank you again and let you know I won't ask you to do this again."

Tory opened her mouth to answer, but Mother's voice came from down the hall. "Mildred, darling, are you almost done?"

"Just the den and ballroom." They were close enough that she could speak the words and she knew her mother would hear. Any farther and her mother would've sent a servant. She must have heard their voices if not their words.

"You can show her next time. The kitchen just finished the lobster bisque. It's ready to be served. Come, join us for dinner."

The two retraced their steps down the hall. This time, they found her parents waiting in the dining room. The table that would fit twelve was set for four. She and Tory took the two empty seats. They sat next to each other across from Mother. Father sat at the head of the table.

The servers immediately placed bowls of lobster bisque and glasses of chardonnay. Albert picked up his glass. "Tory, welcome to our table. Please enjoy the soup and wine."

She shot Mildred a look, eyes wide and questioning.

"It's chardonnay."

After taking a small sip and tasting the soup, a wide smile spread over Tory's face. "This is amazing, thank you."

A look of joy radiated from Mother's face. "I'm glad you like it. Now, tell me, are you thinking of doing more than being a nurse?"

Tory finished off the spoonful of soup she'd scooped. Her face stayed soft and open, as if the question hadn't offended her. "No. I wanted to be a nurse my whole life, and after learning all the dirty secrets of the occupation, I love it even more. Don't get me wrong, it's hard, tiring—a pain some days—but it's in my soul."

A sense of pride filled Mildred at how well Tory handled that first hurdle.

Father nodded as Tory spoke. "So, you see yourself running around the emergency room in ten years, twenty, longer?"

"I think so." Tory shrugged. "I mean, being a nurse means more than one department. I do love the puzzles, but that doesn't mean I won't one day want to switch to something less intense."

"That makes sense. You work nights right now. Is that something you think you want to continue doing?"

Mildred sighed. "Is this the interrogation of Tory hour?"

As they spoke, the soup dishes were cleared, and a server placed a bowl of spicy Thai red fish curry down in front of each of them. A glass of Sauvignon Blanc was matched with the curry.

A smile blossomed across Tory's face as she tasted each. "Amazing."

Conversation shifted to what her parents did as they ate the duck entree, salad, and the coffee course.

Lifting the tiny mug to her mouth, Mildred watched as Tory took a deep breath through her nose before sipping the coffee. She chuckled. "You're as much a coffee connoisseur as you aren't a wine one."

"Truth. This is good coffee. Maybe not the best I've had but in the top five. I approve."

Mother smiled. "Would you like more?"

Tory sighed. "Yes, please."

A servant refilled her mug. She leaned back as if ready to take a nap. Other servers came out carrying individual strawberry Swiss rolls with chocolate bark and pistachio macaron mushrooms. Tory's eyes almost popped from her head as the plate was placed in front of her with a small glass of port wine.

Tory tasted each, and a smile Mildred equated with true pleasure spread on her face. "Wow! This is fantastic. Your cook is really good. You know, I have a friend who can cook, and I get a great meal about once a month. I'll have to tease her that you have someone just about as good as her back there."

Father scoffed. "Our regular cook is excellent, but Priscilla wanted tonight to be special. She called into her favorite restaurant and begged the head cook to work for us for the night. She said 'no.' Then your mother said she'd pay her staff double for the night. Still a 'no.' Triple? That did it. So, we get this famous chef for one night and have to pay her staff triple for the night. She refuses to be paid. Said she wanted to make sure her staff was taken care of, but after their pay was covered three times over, she felt enough had been paid."

As Father told the story, Tory's smile grew. By the end, she covered her mouth, trying not to laugh.

Father's eyes narrow. "Okay, Tory, tell me your joke."

"Well, is the restaurant Ocean Sunrise? Are you talking about the chef, Connie Jax?"

Mildred's jaw dropped.

Mother tilted her head. "Are you telling me that this friend you mentioned is Chef Connie?"

Tory looked over her shoulder towards the kitchen. "Is Connie here?"

"I doubt it. I think she said she'd stay until dinner was done, but then she'd be heading back to the restaurant. It's lovely you know her, though."

They got up and moved to the family room. Once they were all seated on the couches, Mother leaned back and smiled at Tory. "Now, Tory, we need to discuss the holiday season and what we can expect. You are obviously a very busy woman with a tight schedule. We have a weekend retreat in a couple of weeks to wine country, a Thanksgiving soiree, and of course, the Christmas parties. Can I pencil you in for the weekend wine country retreat? It would be good for people to meet Mildred's partner."

Mildred couldn't believe what Mother had asked. She knew this was a second date, and she was already planning both their social calendars? It was unreasonable. Her gut roiled with the impropriety. Fists clenched, she opened her mouth to snap at her, but before she could speak, she heard Tory answer.

"I think I can manage a full weekend if I know early enough in advance. I'll have to do some swaps, but again, I just need advanced warning. Thanksgiving is a big 'no.' At least, not that

Thursday. I have a large family, and I won't miss the family meal. As for the rest, I really think we should play this by ear, don't you?"

Mildred snapped her mouth shut. Was Tory really agreeing to Mother's madness?

Chapter 19 - When Two Wolves Get Together
Tamsin

Tamsin stretched in bed, relaxing before joining the rest of the pack for Sunday brunch. Next to her, Paige still slept. Her jobs as a lifeguard and independent journalist meant she could sleep later than a college instructor.

She leaned over and gave her fiancé a kiss. A warmth filled her with that word. *I can't believe she said 'yes.' I can't believe the question was asked!* Tamsin slapped her hands over her mouth before her laughter bubbled out. Every time she thought about the proposal and the upcoming wedding, a giddiness filled her.

Not wanting to wake Paige, she slipped from bed, and took a quick shower. She dressed in jeans and a T-shirt.

The scent of coffee drew her down the hall to the kitchen. She found Orin and Georgette discussing the morning meal.

"French toast?" Orin suggested.

Georgette sighed. "It takes so long to individually make all those slices. It's early, why not bread pudding? Similar, but we can make several and let them bake all at once."

It was Orin's turn to sigh. "Are you going to take over the sweet bread then?"

"No, that's your duty this week. I'm just trying to make your life easier."

Tamsin poured herself a large mug of Orin's special coffee blend. No one else could create his magical brew. She added a splash of milk and sighed. Heaven. "I'll make the bread pudding, Orin, if you take over the bacon."

He smiled. "Sounds good to me."

She nodded. "Perfect. What other options will be on the table this week?"

Georgette smiled wide. The woman was always happy. "Fruit, oatmeal, bagels, scrambled eggs, and a cheese board."

The three jumped in and started preparing their menu. As they cooked, others came in. Some helped, some watched, depending on their abilities in the kitchen. Tory and Paige sat at the table, drinking coffee and watching.

Paige rubbed her eyes. "I haven't seen you since that fake date of yours. How did it go?"

Tamsin looked up from slicing fruit to watch Tory's reaction. From what she could tell, no one had gotten her story. That was usually Georgette's forte, but Tory'd been working.

After a sigh, and a long pull from her coffee, Tory gave a small smile. "It was okay. I'm still trying to figure it all out. Her parents don't seem to have an issue with her being a lesbian, but Mildred still wants to pretend we're dating."

Paige shook her head. "Still? That wasn't the end?"

Tory grumbled. "There's this thing in a few weeks, an opening to the holiday season. I guess it's always the first weekend in October."

Tamsin's brow rose. "Like the full weekend?"

Both women's heads popped up to gaze at her. Tory nodded. "Yeah. It's in wine country at a resort, I guess. They leave Friday and come back on Monday."

From over by the stove, Orin snorted. "Can you take a full weekend off from work? Four days off? Is that even in your DNA?"

"You're worried about her work?" Paige practically screeched. "She's considering doing a full four days of fake dating!" She turned to Tory. "Have you considered what that would entail?"

Tory slumped. "I have. I think with it being in a resort for so many days, we'll have downtime. Orin's right; I haven't taken time off in years. It will be nice to have some time to relax."

Tamsin chuckled to herself, but it was Paige who answered. "Do you really think you'll be able to relax? You'll be trying to impress not only Mildred's parents, but this society of theirs. You'll need to be dressed to the nines the whole time as well. This won't be a vacation, Tory."

The petite woman shook her head. "I already agreed. Don't worry, I know what I'm doing. It'll be fine."

Before anyone could say anything, Connie joined them. The resident chef worked nights, and like Tory, wasn't seen by many during the week. "What have I missed?"

Orin gave her a kiss and quickly filled her in before heading back to the stove.

She smiled. "The Quincy family loves Tory. They barely know her, but not only did they pay triple to have me cook last Thursday, they had many wonderful things to say about her on Friday when they came to settle the bill. I received a generous tip out of it, too."

This was why Tamsin demanded the weekly brunch. How else could she get all the gossip? Georgette was good, but there was so much more to learn! "You cooked at Tory's fake date?"

Connie laughed. "I did. Mr. and Mrs. Quincy were worried that the blue-haired pixie their daughter brought to the gallery was selected to tweak them. After the dinner, they were thrilled that Mildred had found a sweet, intelligent woman."

Tory groaned as her head fell to her crossed arms. "I don't want to disappoint them."

Leaning across the table, Paige rubbed her shoulder. "Why? You *are* smart and nice."

A low growl came from Tory. "When this all comes to an end, her parents will be disappointed. Maybe we should 'break up' before the weekend."

Connie shook her head, not that Tory could see it. "I wouldn't. I've seen the Quincy's parading men in front of Mildred for years. If you can handle the façade, it would be nice for her to have a friend at the season opener for once. Worry about her, not her parents. They'll survive."

Tory sighed, then finished her coffee. "I just hope I do."

Paige's jaw dropped. "Wait, are you starting to really like this woman?"

With a slightly panicked look on her face, Tory shrugged. "I don't know."

Chapter 20 - The Rules Change ... Again
Tory

"**M**y belly has hurt for a few days. Now, before you go thinking it's my appendix, I had that out when I was five. So, it's not that."

Tory smiled at the older woman lying in the bed. Concern in his eyes, her husband sat in a chair.

"She started complaining about the pain two days ago, but it was much sharper yesterday. She didn't want to come here. I insisted." His voice was gravelly and a bit moist with age. "She never thinks anything is really wrong with her."

"The doctor will be here soon. Is there anything else you need before I head out?"

The woman's eyes narrowed. "I'm in pain, and my mouth is dry. Won't you give me anything for the pain? Can I get some water? I thought you people were here to help me feel better, not worse."

Closing up the medical record, Tory smiled at her. "We can't give you medicine without knowing exactly what's wrong with you. As for the water, if we need to do a procedure, then your stomach needs to be empty. I'll see if we can get an IV with saline going if you're feeling thirsty."

Tory walked out of the room and went to the nurses' station.

Dwight flopped in a chair a few moments later. "Patient in room seven. Twins. Both crying." Tory could hear the ruckus. "The parents saw a raisin go up the nose of one of them, but by the time they got here, they weren't sure which one. Can I tell you how much fun that was?"

Tory couldn't stop the smile that spread across her face. "I'm sure. Tons of fun. This is why you keep talking about your future kids, right?"

"God above, stop. Never."

"You know, one day, you're going to meet your match. Find the man of your dreams, fall in love ... and he's going to want kids."

Dwight bent over, hands on knees, gasping for breath. "Do not speak with the devil's tongue, woman!"

Tory laughed as she swung around to finish up her notes. Dr. Aimes stopped behind the counter. "Dwight, you can start the discharge for the twins. Send them home. Tory, I'm about to head into room three."

She looked up from her notes. "Watch out for that couple. They're going to try to sneak something for her to drink or eat. I put in an order for an X-ray and possible **MRI**, they just need your signature."

He nodded and entered the room.

Next to her, Dwight logged off his computer. "It's been a few days. You've been swapping for that first weekend in October. A full weekend off, m'dear. What are you doing?"

She shook her head. "Nothing."

"Does this have to do with that mystery date you finally went on last Thursday—a date with our esteemed leader?"

Her jaw dropped. "How did you know? I didn't tell anyone, and there's no way she would've said anything."

"Honey, Dwight knows everything. When are you going to learn this? You may as well spill."

"Did you just refer to yourself in third person? And you expect me to trust you?"

He laughed. "Fine. I don't know everything, but I have a friend who knows Mildred's parents. They heard about the dinner ... and that you're going to the season opener in October. So, dish, woman. You and Mildred?"

Tory blushed. She didn't know what to say. The more she thought about the other woman, the more her heart and belly did a small soft shoe dance within her. "I'm just trying to help her out. Her parents keep setting her up on dates. I'm trying to give her a friend to take to these events, so they stop."

Dwight's eyes narrowed, then he shook his head. "No, it's more than that. You like her."

"What? Why do you say that?"

"Girl, I'm an expert. This is what I do. I have two specialties in life. One: I'm an excellent nurse, and two: I can smell relationships a mile away."

Tory opened her mouth to put him in his place when the phone for the ambulance sounded. She glared at him and ran, not bothering to get the information.

Over the radio, she heard the symptoms for a heart attack. As the driver leapt from the cab of the truck she asked, "Did the patient come from the homeless encampment?"

"No, she was at the open market north of the city. One of the booth owners saw her fall."

The doors opened, and the young woman was placed on a stretcher. As Tory ran with the team that wanted to save the young woman, she cataloged the new facts for this heart attack victim: young woman, herbal and earthy scent—witch.

Chapter 21 - Who Called the Cops?
Mildred

The piles on Mildred's desk never seemed to go down no matter how much she picked away at them. She was convinced there were evil spirits who came in at night and added to the stacks of paper. With a sigh, she drank more of her morning coffee, and moved on to staff evaluations. They had to be done quarterly for new employees, biannually for anyone who'd worked at the hospital for two to five years, and yearly for everyone else.

She and Andy swapped the reports every quarter, and it was her turn. She was about to dive in when someone knocked on her door. More than happy with the distraction, she pushed the pile away. "Come in."

Andy came in, a wide smile on his face and a coffee cup in his hand. He'd taken a week-long vacation, traveling to visit family in Delaware. She was thrilled to see him back. "Hiya, stranger, long time no see."

He lifted his cup in salute. "I would say it's nice to be back, but my vacation was too nice to lie."

"I get that. I think all this—" she waved at the piles of paper on her desk, "—is really yours. Someone decided to prank me and give me all your work while you were away."

"I paid quite heavily for that service, I'll have you know." He grinned. "But, even if I'd like to still be back home, it's nice to see you. How was the family dinner last week? I can't believe I've missed all the drama!"

"No drama. Dinner was good. Mother put together an excellent menu, as always. You know how it goes."

"It's been years since I've had dinner at your family's estate. You know, you could always pretend we're dating."

"They wouldn't believe it."

"True. But at least invite me over there for dinner when your mother is putting on an event. I'm drooling just thinking about it."

Mildred laughed. "Okay, I'll see what I can arrange."

"How was spending the evening with Tory?"

"The night went well. My parent's love her." *And I ... like her. Even before any of this happened, I imagined finding a woman like her, full of sass and vinegar. Someone who would challenge me. Now that I've gotten to know her, she is also funny and smart ...* Mildred shook her head, bringing herself back into the present.

"Is that good or bad?"

"They invited her to the season opener."

Andy's jaw dropped. "To wine country? The full weekend even of who's who?"

Mildred nodded, biting her lip. "Yeah, that."

"How are you getting out of that?"

"That's just it. Tory agreed to do it. She seems to want to let me get out of my parent's ministrations."

Andy leaned back. "Tell me the truth, Mil. Is there anything there?"

She took a sip of coffee, considering what to say. Before she could answer, her phone rang. She picked up the receiver. "Quincy."

"Hi, Mil, it's Brandy. We have a meeting in thirty with the police. I'd like both you and Andy, if he's still around."

Mildred's gut tensed at her boss's words. She didn't have much contact with Dr. Brandy Ava, but when the woman called, Mildred came to attention. The other woman rose in the ranks at the hospital fast, and everyone who worked for her respected her for her integrity and leadership.

Focusing on Andy, she waved him over to let him know he should listen in. She said to Dr. Ava, "The police? Why are we having a meeting with the police?"

"They want to discuss what's been happening with the weird string of deaths. They have some officers looking into the heart attacks and want our research."

"Who's coming to the meeting?"

There was a pause. "It will be me, Dr. Tells, you, Andy, and one of the emergency room nurses. I spoke to Dennis. He suggested a nurse who's been taking notes on cases coming in for a few weeks."

Mildred sighed. The nurse had to be Tory. How had her life come to this? Tory was popping up everywhere. "You mean Nurse Byrd?"

She could hear shuffling over the phone, as Andy began to smirk. Mildred rolled her eyes. "Yes, that's it. Tory Byrd. Dennis said she's been keeping records of a run of strange cases coming through the emergency department. I think that'd help the police."

"Okay, I'll see if Andy can join us—" he nodded emphatically, "—and send you a text. Either way, I'll see you at ten."

"Sounds perfect, see you then."

Once she hung up, she kicked Andy out of her office until the meeting. She had to get some work done, but it was hard to concentrate. He knocked on her door five minutes before they had to be there with a new cup of coffee, and she debated her women-only rule. He winked, and they headed off together.

The conference room didn't feel like it belonged in a hospital. It was long and wide with abstract paintings along the wall. Windows looking out over the busy street and parking lot lined the other side. It wasn't the nicest view, but the sun coming in was lovely. The room was taken up by a long oak table stained a dark color. There were a half dozen seats on either side.

In one of the leather rolling chairs on the opposite side sat Dwight with Tory next to him. She sat tall—well, as tall as she could given her petite stature—with a legal pad and a stack of papers in front of her.

At the head of the table sat Dr. Henley Tells, Mildred's other boss. On Dr. Tells's left, and next to Tory, sat Brandy.

Brandy smiled wide. "You found Andy, excellent. Why don't you two sit on this side with us? I want to get fully caught up before the officers get here. They're due in about ten minutes."

After sitting, Andy and Tory gave a run-down of Tory's findings over the last couple of months. *I guess Andy really did know about Tory's findings.*

Both Brandy and Henley leaned back. Henley's brow furrowed. He was about to ask a question when an orderly led in the two officers. One was tall with red hair, the other shorter and rounder.

"Officers Ezra and Flint. They're here to discuss a new case with you." The orderly said before turning and walking out.

They sat, and the bigger man, Officer Ezra, smiled. "We've been tracking a series of heart attacks. We know that it's a natural diagnosis, but the frequency of occurrences is beyond statistically normal. It's happening in all the hospitals around town. We were hoping we could discuss your findings, figure out if you have any information you can add to our investigation."

There was a moment where no one moved. The idea of the case seemed ludicrous. Then all the medical staff turned to Tory. Mildred wanted to laugh; she could only imagine what everyone was thinking. Their expert had blue hair and looked like a teenager, but she'd noticed a pattern in the deaths while others believed it was nothing.

She really is amazing.

Chapter 22 - One Bed - It's a Thing
Tory

Mildred picked up Tory from the pack house. They'd discussed other meeting places, but there was a suitcase involved, and it just made more sense.

"You teased me about how large my parents' house is, and you live here? Do *you* ever get lost in *that* monstrosity?" Mildred teased as Tory clicked her seatbelt into place.

"All the time." She looked over her shoulder at the sprawling den where most of the pack wolves lived. "The difference is, this isn't just me and my family, there are several families living here."

Mildred pulled into traffic. "Like a commune?"

"Yeah, something like that."

The other woman's eyes narrowed. "Or a cult? You aren't in some new-age cult are you? I'd just decided you were smart, and that doesn't jive."

Tory chuckled. "Actually, I believe studies have shown that a lot of people associated with cults are very intelligent."

An eyebrow rose in disagreement at her response, and Tory laughed. She relented, "Okay, fine, not a cult. Where I live is closer to a commune. A bunch of us living in peace with each other and the land." She tilted her head and thought about it. "Usually in peace with each other. There are enough people that ... well, you know."

It was Mildred's turn to laugh. "How did you end up living in a commune, of all places?"

She shrugged. "It's where I grew up. When I returned to Santa Cruz, I just went home."

"Wait, they let you leave?"

Tory shook her head and rolled her eyes. "I told you, it isn't a cult. Of course we can leave if we want to."

"Okay, good. Not a place that holds you prisoner."

Tory relaxed for the ride. "Is there anything I should know about this weekend?" She was excited to get to know Mildred better, and a bit worried. Every time she learned more about the dynamic woman, the more she wanted to learn. She didn't want to lose her heart to someone she was fake-dating. It wouldn't end well—not for her.

"Not really. Knowing my parents, we'll be put in two different wings of the resort. They're all about propriety. There will be social gatherings both during the day and at night. Mornings will be ours to do with as we please." Mildred's voice trailed off as she navigated some thick traffic. "All in all, it should be fun and relaxing."

"That doesn't sound too bad. A free weekend in wine country. That's something new." She smiled and shimmied her shoulders in excitement.

"I'm glad you're excited. I've been doing this my whole life. It'll be fun to see it out of someone else's eyes."

They spent the rest of the drive discussing childhood adventures in school, favorite subjects, and mishaps. By the time they reached the resort, they were laughing like old friends. Tory put her hand on Mildred's arm before they got out of the car. "You know, thanks for this. I haven't had a break in years, or a new friend. I really needed this. I didn't even realize how much. The idea of relaxing in a private room and reading a book ... it sounds beyond divine."

Mildred's face lit up, and Tory's heart skipped a beat. "I'm glad. I didn't want this to be all about me. You're doing me a favor. Having to dodge all the men my parents throw me has been a chore. I can only imagine who they'd find now they know I like women." She paused. "If we're really going to pull this off, there's one more thing. People who know me well call me Mil, not Mildred. You should do that."

Tory paused, mouthing the shorter version of her name, then nodded. "Sounds good."

They got out of the car and gathered their bags. Mildred had called her mother once they were a few minutes away. When they entered the resort, the woman was there, waiting for them. "Mildred, Tory, I'm so glad you're here. I have the key to your room!"

Room? As in singular?

She shot a glance at Mildred and saw the same wide-eyed look of shock on her face. "Thanks, Mother. I had assumed you'd get us two rooms."

"I knew how great the two of you were together. Your father and I aren't old fuddy-duddies! Go, check out the room. It overlooks the vineyards. One of the best at the resort; I made sure of it."

Tory could tell Mildred forced a smile. "That's great, Mother, thanks." She took the key card as a resort worker gathered the bags and then led them towards their room.

The room was exquisite. The designers had decorated it in whites, tans, and light blues. The far wall was floor-to-ceiling windows, with light curtains billowing in the cool breeze. To the left of the door sat a small table with two overstuffed chairs and a loveseat. A few feet from the sitting area was a mahogany desk, long enough to support two chairs. On the opposite wall there was a full kitchen, bigger than Tory's apartment in Texas.

Between the sitting area and desk there was a door, and behind the kitchen another door.

Tory watched Mildred tip the porter before he left. She smiled. "Which door first?"

"Let's go to the left."

They found an in-floor hot tub bubbling with steam rising from it. Along the wall hung towels and plush white robes with the resort's logo on the chest. Benches lined the other wall as well as a small television. The ceiling and opposite wall were windows overlooking rows and rows of grape vines.

For a moment, Tory forgot to breathe. "This is ... I don't even have words. Can we spend the weekend in here?"

Mildred laughed. "The others may be suspicious."

They walked to the other door and discovered the bedroom. A spacious room with two dressers, a large window letting in the same cool breeze from the great room, and two more doors. Tory checked over her shoulder to make sure, but this was it. "There's only one bed."

Mildred nodded. "I'll sleep on the couch."

"It's too small, even for me."

"It's fine, I'll manage."

"Look at the bed. It's huge. I think we can figure out a way to share it."

Mildred stared at her. "Are you sure? I've already dragged you here. I don't want to make this any more awkward than it already is."

Tory smiled. "I'm sure. We're friends. It'll be fine, I'm sure."

Chapter 23 - Welcome to Society
Mildred

Mildred watched Tory, trying to figure out if everything was too much. The resort, her parents, a shared room, a shared bed—but so far the other woman seemed to be taking things in stride. She wasn't sure why Tory was so chill, but she was thankful for it.

She quickly checked out the two remaining doors of their room for the weekend. An en suite bathroom, larger than what she had with her apartment. A full shower for two, a toilet and bidet, double sinks, and a bathtub. It was all spacious and done in white and light blue, with a few accents of dark blue. Thankfully, it had a closing door. The other door was a walk-in closet.

I've never been in one of the rooms this big before. This must be a newlywed suite with the jacuzzi.

Behind her, Tory whistled. "Can I move in here? This is luxury at its best. I didn't see your room in the palace where your parents lived, so you may be used to this ... but wow!"

"Oh, no! I had some fancy things, but this is over-the-top—even for me."

They moved their bags to the suitcase holder in the room. Mildred saw a sheet of paper on the desk and went over to read over the itinerary for the weekend. "There's a dinner tonight. Over the next few days there are some activities everyone is expected to attend, and some options."

Tory came and looked over her shoulder. "A tour of the facilities. Oh! Look, we can stomp on grapes to experience the old-fashioned way wine was made. That sounds ... messy, but fun. It's a competition. Winner wins a bottle of wine, who could've guessed."

Mildred smiled. "There's a horseback ride into the hills on Sunday, or a hike if you'd prefer."

Tory read over all the options. "How many things are we expected to do, and how many events with your parents?"

"Those are good questions. The dinners are big social affairs. Everyone goes. Beyond that, it's more of a scene to be seen. They've set up all of the other things on this list because there are enough kids, teens, and people in their twenties and thirties, that they've realized we need to get out and on our own, or there will be social mishaps."

"Are there stories from the before times?" Tory waggled her brows. "Some big to-dos when parents demanded their kids stay and behave?"

"No, but I could make some up." She thought about how she could embellish some of her adventures with the people she hung out with over the years.

With a sigh, Tory spun and walked to a chair. "That's fine. How long do we have until dinner, and do I have to dress up?"

Mildred checked the clock on the desk. "About an hour, and yes. All social events will be formal, unfortunately."

"No worries. Do you mind if I jump in the shower?"

"Not at all."

Forty-five minutes later, they were both ready to go. Tory wore a wine-colored dress. The bodice was fitted to her waist. The skirt fell to just below her knees. Mildred wore a peach, long-sleeved wrap dress with small black and white flowers on it.

In the great hall, they found Mildred's parents. Mother beamed at them, coming over to give each a quick hug, kissing first Mildred and then Tory on their cheeks. "You both look perfect. Tonight will be excellent. The meal will be small, so eat up now."

A server walked by with petite cucumber sandwiches. They each took one.

As they slowly made their way to the table, Mildred watched as Tory gaped at all the people. Everyone came dressed to impress. Shiny new tuxedos, jewel colored dresses. The bling outshone the chandeliers hanging from the ceiling.

Mother's idea of a small meal and Mildred's were different. The menu included a soup course, salad, fish, lamb, and ended with cheesecake. Each course had been paired with a wine from the resort. They sat at the table with Mildred's family's best friends, the Barclays. They'd been part of Mildred's circle of friends her entire life.

Despite the number of people in the room—both the people sitting and enjoying the meal, and the servers in the black slacks and white button-down shirts, ensuring everyone was content with their meal—their table felt cozy. Everyone could talk and joke freely.

Astor, a couple years older than her, lifted his glass to Tory. "About time someone broke through Mildred's inability to commit. I never thought *anyone* would get through her zone of avoidance."

Mother narrowed her eyes at him. "You knew our Mildred liked girls?"

Sarah, the youngest of the Barclay children, sighed. "Women, Mrs. Quincy. Once we have to wear a bra, we're no longer girls."

"Fine. Women. Astor Barclay, you knew Mildred liked *women* and you let me continue to find men for her? You even helped me find some of the poor saps."

Mildred groaned. "You didn't!"

Astor lifted his wine glass in salute and waggled his brows. "Of course, I did. If you weren't going to help her, I was going to have a good laugh."

Branson, the middle child, rolled his eyes. He spent most of his life with his nose in a book, and probably didn't even realize he was at a social event. "Astor was probably hoping one of the men would look at him and decide to change teams."

Astor threw his head back and laughed. "You aren't wrong, brother, but I'm fine with the women I'm dating, as well. Maybe I'll find a couple who'll take me in like a long-lost pet."

His father practically snarled. "You'll do no such thing. You'll behave, is what you'll do. I don't care if you like men or women, just choose one and settle down."

Next to her, Mildred saw Tory biting her lip, trying not to laugh. This fight wasn't new, but Mildred could see the humor in it if it was the first time you'd experienced it.

Astor leaned in. "What do you two say; you have that big jacuzzi in your room. How about we leave the older generation to their stodgy ways and slip into that steamy water."

Mildred narrowed her eyes. "You *will* be wearing a swimsuit, right?"

"If I have to."

Sarah smiled. "I'm in!" She leapt up and headed for the door.

Branson shook his head. "Not me. I'm going to go read and sleep. You can have fun staying up all night, but I just want to survive this weekend."

Mildred and Tory said their goodnights to her parents and headed to their room. They changed, and moments later both Sarah and Astor showed up at the door, Astor with a couple of bottles of the resort's best Cabernet Sauvignon.

Mildred rolled her eyes. "We've all already had enough, don't you think?"

Astor shook his head. "We're at a vineyard, Mildred; it's never enough. Now, into the bubbly warm water. It's time to relax."

Once they all sat in the hot tub, somehow each with their own bottle of wine, Astor smiled wickedly. "Okay, now for the fun. Drink if you've ever kissed a woman."

Everyone drank.

"Drink if you've ever kissed a man."

Again, everyone took a drink.

Astor smirked. "Drink if you've done more than kiss a woman."

This time Sarah didn't drink. She shrugged when Astor looked at her. "The kiss wasn't that good, why would I do more?"

He nodded at that. "Fair enough. Will you try again, or are you men only from now on?"

"I don't know. Maybe if the right woman comes along."

Astor gazed at everyone in the tub. "Drink if you've done more than kiss a bloke."

This time Tory was the only one who didn't drink. Astor raised an eyebrow at her. She smiled wide at him. "You're expecting my secrets? You think you've gotten me drunk enough for that?"

"If not, pretty lady, drink more. There is a story there, and I want it."

She laughed and took a long pull from her bottle of wine. When the bottle came down, her eyes danced. "Let's just say, I've never met a man who intrigued me as much as a woman."

Astor leaned forward. "If you weren't here with Mildred, so much like a sister to me, I may take that as a challenge."

"Yeah, don't think I didn't know what you were doing, asking questions with me being the only one you don't know. But that's fine. I'm learning about all of you, too."

Sarah shook her head. "We could all just drink. I doubt there's enough wine to get the new girl to kiss you, brother."

Tory snorted. "Is that what this is all about? Trying to get the new girl to kiss you?"

"Was there ever a doubt?" Astor winked at her.

"I don't think there's enough wine in my bottle." Tory lifted it up in salute, then tipped her bottle back to drink.

Astor handed her his. "You can finish mine."

With a sigh, Sarah pulled herself from the water. "It's late, Ash. Why don't we leave these two to their first night in paradise? They don't need us here."

"Fine." He followed his sister. "But we'll be back here tomorrow. This was fun."

Once they left, Tory put the bottle down and giggled. "Oh! I'm glad Sar—" She stopped to take a breath and started over. "Sar ... rah! Took him away. I'm a bit tipsy." Tory put action to words and started slipping to her right.

Mildred quickly slid to Tory's side before she went under. "You okay?"

Tory gazed up at her. "You're really pretty, did you know that? And smart. And pretty."

"And you're drunk." This relaxed tipsy version of Tory was cute.

"Can't get drunk, not me."

"Everyone can get drunk." Amusement fought with the shock and momentary hope Mildred had felt at Tory's words. "Let's get you into bed."

A wide smile spread on Tory's face. "You wanna have your way with me, sexy lady?" She leaned in and pressed her lips to Mildred's.

For a moment, heat flashed through her, and Mildred returned the kiss. It had been too long and the kiss ... gah, it felt good. A low moan from Tory brought Mildred to her senses and she pulled away.

Tory sighed. "I guess you liking me back was too much to hope for." She crawled from the hot tub, pushed herself to her feet, and wobbled her way across the living room.

Mildred debated following her, but she seemed to be walking well enough. *I'll give her time to change and get into bed. She and I can discuss the kiss tomorrow, when she's sober.*

She touched her lips, which still tingled from the contact with the sassy woman. With a glance over her shoulder, her heart pounded harder. *What if I do like you? What if I want that kiss to happen again?*

Chapter 24 - I kissed a Girl? Do tell ...
Tory

The resort room with all its windows letting in all the sun was amazing, until Tory wanted to sleep in. She didn't have a hangover, her wolf ate pain for breakfast, but she ached with fatigue. *What the hell happened last night? How did I get into bed?*

She rolled over and saw Mildred sleeping next to her, the beautiful woman curled up on her side facing away. Tory looked down and saw she still wore her bikini. *Why didn't I change out of this damned thing?* Checking around, she saw a bath towel tangled in with the blankets on the bed. *What the fuck happened? Astor asked questions. I drank my wine and some of his. For fuck's sake, how much alcohol can I drink without getting drunk? Apparently not over a bottle.*

She grabbed some clean clothes, then went to the bathroom to shower. The warm water sluiced away the anxiety of not remembering the end of the night. *Did I say or do anything I shouldn't have?* An uncomfortable talk with Mildred loomed.

She used the fancy scented shampoo and soap. It was so expensive, the aroma didn't offend her nose. Once clean, she put on a pale yellow button-down shirt and blue skirt.

Outside of the bathroom, she found Mildred sitting up in the bed, awake. She gave the other woman a sheepish smile. "Hey, I'm sorry if I did anything last night. I remember Astor handing me his bottle of wine, but after that, nothing much. Did I do anything embarrassing? I usually can drink a lot of alcohol without it affecting me. I'm not used to getting drunk."

Mildred gave her an odd look. Then she gazed off into the distance. "No, nothing embarrassing. Astor and Sarah left, and we headed to bed."

"Are you sure nothing weird happened?" Tory forced a laugh.

After a moment, Mildred pointed at the list on the table. "Have you decided what you want to do today? We can order breakfast here or go to the dining room for a buffet. Why don't you look over the list while I take a quick shower?"

Tory couldn't read the weird tension but appreciated the subject change. "Sure, I'll come up with my top three and you can decide what you want to do, too. This isn't just about me."

"No worries, you can just decide what you want."

Before Tory could say anything more, the bathroom door closed.

Once Mildred was done, they decided they'd go to breakfast, then head out for a hike. After lunch, they'd do the grape-stomping competition.

Tory knew she must've done something, Mildred was acting weird, quiet and withdrawn. *Did I say or do something last night? We've all been trained not to talk about pack, so I doubt it was that, but ... she was so pretty last night. I ... there's no way. Maybe she just needed coffee.* Even Tory could feel the desperate hope in her thoughts.

The buffet wasn't like any Tory had ever seen. The beginning had eggs, bacon, sausage, and ham. The middle had personally made pancakes, French toast, and waffles. Extras were added by personal preference. The next station had steaks and omelets prepared by request. At the last station, a server shaved succulent slices from a prime rib roast for people.

How many chefs work at this resort?

Tory wanted it all. She decided then and there that, next time, she'd come down early and start before anyone knew, so she could eat enough for three or four.

Next to her, Mildred moaned in happiness. "This is my favorite meal. I'm going to request a skirt steak, and then get a plate of food. If you want, I can put in an order for you, too."

A groan grumbled deep in Tory's throat. "Yes, please. And fried eggs, if they'll do it. I could eat everything here ... twice."

Mildred huffed out a laugh, then looked her up and down. "Not that I'm arguing your statement, but I'd love to see that level of gluttony from you, my friend."

Tory winked. "Don't tempt me."

As Mildred sauntered away, a wave of relief washed through Tory. Their exchange felt more relaxed than any other that morning. *Maybe I imagined it all and nothing happened last night.*

Tory headed towards the sweet section and requested blueberry pancakes. Once she had a stack, she covered the lovelies with fresh berries and syrup. From the meat table, she added bacon. She selected a clean plate and piled it with hash browns, a pepper medley, and more fresh fruit. After setting her plates on a table, she headed back to find coffee. Mildred was at the table with a less mountainous amount of food when she returned.

"Whoa!" Mildred said, eyes wide. "You weren't kidding. I should snap a photo for the hospital Instagram page. 'Will she finish it all?' Let people vote."

Tory snorted before starting in on her food.

The two sat in companionable silence as they ate.

"My gods, this is delicious! I can see why you love this meal."

Mildred tilted her head. "Gods? As in, more than one?"

"Yeah, I'm not that religious, but if pushed, I'd pray to the Greek gods. Artemis being my favorite."

"Oh! That's interesting. I've never heard of people believing in a multi-god pantheon."

Tory ducked her head and shrugged. She hadn't meant to get into this discussion. She took another bite of the skirt steak, enjoying the delicious flavor. Moving on to the hashbrowns, she discovered the cooks had added something to the mix that had her taste buds dancing. *Gods! Have I died and gone to food heaven?* She couldn't believe how good it tasted.

"Do you do anything to honor your gods?"

Mildred's questions pulled Tory away from the wonders of the food she ate. "Um, maybe. I love honoring the full moon. Once a month, I try to do something to respect her."

Mildred's fork stopped halfway to her mouth. "Is that why you don't work on full moon nights?"

Tory bit her lip. She'd hoped no one had noticed, but apparently Mildred had. "Ah, yeah. That, and to avoid the craziest of the crazies!"

"If you'd put it down as a religious reason, then you wouldn't have to swap, you know."

"That's more complicated. It's fine the way I'm doing it now."

A single brow rose. "If you insist. I just think it's really interesting."

Tory went to sip her coffee, but realized it was empty. *Stupid small mug.* "Want a refill?" she asked Mildred, as she stood up to refill her own.

"Sure, thanks."

She loved how comfortable their conversation had been, but she knew something weird had happened the previous night. When she returned, she finally decided she had to know. "Tell me what stupid thing I did last night. I know there was something."

"No."

"What? What do you mean, 'no?'"

Mildred shut her eyes then rubbed her face. "I mean, you don't want to know. Let's just leave it in the past."

"Unless I ran around naked—and even then I probably won't care—just tell me."

The other woman leaned forward, pointing at Tory with her fork. "You wouldn't care if you ran around this place naked?"

Tory scrunched up her face and debated her answer. "I mean, it probably would be hard on you, and this weekend isn't about making your life harder. But beyond that, probably not. Nudity doesn't bother me."

"What if I told you you hit on me?"

Tory felt her face heat up. *When was the last time I flirted with anyone? Why haven't I been flirting with hot women? When I get back to Santa Cruz, I'm going to demand Georgette take me out again so I can socialize. It's obviously been too long.* "Well, how far did I go? Was it more than telling you you're cute?"

It was Mildred's turn to blush. "You said I was pretty, and you kissed me."

Damn it. I miss all the good things in my life! Stupid wine. "Was it good? I mean, it's been a long time since I've kissed anyone, and I don't remember." She gave a bit of a desperate and hopeful smile, trying to lessen the awkwardness of the conversation. She knew she probably failed.

Mildred laughed. "Well, if you play your cards right, maybe you can have a do-over when you can remember it."

Tory's eyes widened. "Deal."

They stared at each other for another few seconds. Tory wondered if her face was turning as many shades of red as Mildred's. Then she bent to her food and focused on eating.

The weather was beautiful as was the land the resort owned. They walked in silence, but once the hike began it wasn't awkward. The views were amazing. Along the five mile circular path were boards giving facts about the vineyard and its history. It traveled up for a bit, and after an hour they found an overlook that let them see the full resort: buildings, rows of plants, and all. It was breathtaking.

At one point, the path opened up to a view of the fields of trees.

Mildred pointed to a bench. "Want to take a break?"

"Sure, it's beautiful out here, and we're not in any hurry."

The cool of the shade and the beauty around them seeped into Tory. *This would be a fantastic place to run as a wolf. If it wasn't so populated. I wonder if Tamsin could rent it out one weekend.* Sniffing the air, she could almost feel the breeze in her fur as she chased the scents on the breeze.

She shook herself, bringing herself back to the present. She closed her eyes and thought about everything that had happened over the last few weeks. The gallery event, dinner at Mildred's parents place, and agreeing to this silly weekend. *Why am I doing this? Is it just to help my boss? Or is my heart, my soul, my wolf, pushing me towards something I'm blindly ignoring?*

She leaned back as she thought about the woman sitting beside her. Mildred was beautiful and smart, but also her boss. *Gods above, what am I thinking? This could never work.*

Then again ... nothing ventured and all that. If she didn't take a step forward, she'd never know. She'd always be in the same place ... without a partner or in love.

Her heart pounded harder in her chest. As she got up the nerve to speak, her mouth dried and betrayed her, the words unwilling to form.

Why am I so nervous? What's the worst thing that could happen? We end up right where we are? Stop being afraid, Tory. Take a breath and talk to the woman next to you.

She pushed herself upright and turned to face Mildred. The other woman sat with her legs stretched out, crossed at her ankles, leaning back on her hands. She smiled back at Tory. "Did you have a question for me?"

Tory licked her lips. "Yeah. I've enjoyed our fake dating time together." She stopped. Why was this so hard?

Mildred sat up, crossing her legs. "But you want to stop the farce?"

"Yes. Well, no." Tory put her hands up between them. "I just ... I want to stop the 'fake' part. I like what I've learned about you since we've been spending time together. I'd like to try this out for real." She bit her lower lip, dropping her hands and looking down. It occurred to her that she should've waited until the end of the weekend to do this. Her voice lowered as she continued. "If you don't want to make it real, I won't ruin this for you. I mean, I get it, I'm—"

A finger under her chin lifted her face up to the other woman's. Mildred's dark eyes danced. "You're what, Tory? Smart? Sassy? Funny? Sexy? I gave up trying to date when several times a month my parents threw some random guy at me. It seemed like too much work. When you offered to pretend to be my girlfriend, I thought it would be convenient. I had no idea just who you were and how ..." She stopped talking and leaned down, pressing her soft lips to Tory's.

Mind a jumble of shock and excitement, Tory lifted a hand, weaving her fingers into Mildred's short dark hair. She probed her tongue into the other woman's mouth. She tasted of syrup and cinnamon.

One of Mildred's arms wound around her neck, as the other encircled her waist.

Tory's hand moved down to Mildred's shoulder, and started to move lower when the sound of a snapping twig shocked her from the kiss. The two of them jerked apart.

"Don't let me stop you." Astor said, walking up the trail, a wide grin on his face. "Please, continue. You two make a much better view than the vineyard."

Mildred stood, then rolled her eyes. "What are you doing here, Astor?"

"It's a hiking trail, Mildred. What do you think I'm doing? I'm hiking. Did you think it was a private trail?" He was the only one who chuckled. "If I'd waited ten minutes would the show have been better?"

Tory stood and slid her hand into Mildred's. "Let's continue on the path. I still want to do the grape-stomping this afternoon."

Astor called after them as they walked down the path. "And, Mil, your parents are looking for you. Don't forget about them."

Face scrunching up in ire, she shrugged. "Oh, well, so much for our morning off. Time to socialize."

Tory winked at her. "Time to be wonderful."

Astor laughed as the three of them continued down the path.

Chapter 25 - Don't Stomp on Me
Mildred

Sarah bounced ahead of them, excited for the competition. "I've been wanting to do this for ages. They stopped doing this a few years back, and no one under twenty-one was allowed to participate. I never could compete. I'm totally taking the prize this year!"

Mildred laughed at her exuberance. "I'm sure you are."

Next to her, Tory's mouth quirked up in a small smile. Mildred gazed at the petite woman, still astonished by their earlier conversation. How had their arrangement become real? They'd been on two dates, and now, all of a sudden, it wasn't a game anymore.

I've been admiring Tory since before the gallery. I guess now I can truly explore my feelings. She shook her head, wondering if she'd dreamed it all.

"I'm so going to beat her," Tory said softly. "I may be small, but I can move like the wind."

Mildred laughed, a lightness suffusing her inner being that she hadn't felt in years.

Astor, walking behind them, spoke softly to his brother Brason. Mildred glared at him over her shoulder. "What are you two talking about?"

"Nothing you need to worry about."

Tory sighed and spoke softly. "They're betting on which one of the two of us will do better. Astor put his money on Sarah. Branson thinks I'm hiding something, and is willing to bet on me, if only to shut Astor up."

Mildred's eyebrow flew up her forehead. "Well, that all tracks. How did you hear them?"

"I have good hearing?"

"If you insist, but that's more than good hearing." *That's fantastic hearing. I couldn't hear any of that.*

Tory bumped shoulders with Mildred, shaking her from her thoughts. "The idea of winning the wine makes me happy. Astor losing this bet is just icing on the cake."

They reached the competition site, laughing. There were six old-fashioned washtub barrels set up. Competitors had to sign up early. Tory walked up to the one with her name on it. She had worn a skirt that morning, and it was short enough the judges said it'd work for what she would be doing.

Each of the competitors were asked to wash their feet. There was a glass under a spigot that reached over a foot out from the bottom of the barrel. The officiant spoke to the crowd, though Mildred and Tory had read the rules earlier in the day.

"Each of our four competitors will enter their barrel of grapes. Using nothing but their feet, they'll stomp down to mash the juice from the fruit. The first person to fill the glass will win an exclusive twenty-thirteen bottle of our wine, one of our best years."

Everyone clapped.

"If the four competitors would please step up to the side of the barrel." The barrels were about two feet tall and had a step-stool to help the contestants step in. A wood bar stretched across all the barrels just above waist-height to help with stability.

The announcer, one of the vineyard workers, continued. "Please climb inside. Don't start stomping until the whistle is blown. The judges can see what you're doing." A group of Mildred's parent's friends stood from a table where they sat and waved to cheers. "Anyone starting early will be disqualified. Though the glasses have lines, the winner will be judged based on the weight of the wine." The announcer indicated a scale on the judges table.

Tory and Sarah climbed in their separate barrels. Sarah, almost six feet tall, stood tall and proud. She smirked at the other competitors, and then out towards the crowd. She had a look that said she knew she'd win. *She really believes it, but I agree with Branson. My money's on Tory ... that's if I were to bet.*

Around her, people started placing bets. From the sounds of it, Tory was a very long shot. Branson, true to his word, placed a second bet on her with a bookie. He whispered to Astor, "Why not? She deserves some support, and our bet doesn't count."

Mildred shook her head and waited to see what would happen.

Finally, the whistle blew, and the crowd cheered. Then all you could hear was stomping and squishing. It was horrible and hilarious. There were cameras that each of the individual judges held so the crowd could see what was happening. The camera pointing at Tory's barrel showed her small frame moving quickly. She might be petite, but the woman could move.

The glasses began to fill. They all filled at roughly the same rate. Then Astor yelled out, "Sarah, you're letting Mil's girlfriend beat you. She's half your size!"

Both Tory and Sarah increased their exertions. Before long, the juice in the glasses was nearing the line. Sarah's reached the line first, but the weight wasn't enough. Suddenly, the bell rang and a green light went off over Tory's barrel.

The crowd cheered, but none louder than Mildred. A few people who'd put a lot of money into the bets groaned.

Tory's hands grasped the bar over the barrels as she propelled herself out, landing next to her winning glass of squished grape juice. Her legs, skirt, and shirt were splattered, but her face was radiant. Mildred ran forward and hugged her, not caring if she got messy. "That was fantastic!" Then, at the urging of her friends, leaned down for a kiss.

Chapter 26 - What Wine Pairs with Fish Tacos?
Tory

Tory sat on a stool in the bathroom trying to apply makeup. She didn't put the stuff on often, but tonight was the last hurrah of the weekend, and she knew she had to look her best. She wore a fitted black dress with sparkly beads covering her from the waist up. The skirt, which spun out when she twirled, had fewer of the shiny bits that, if one looked closely, made small flowers.

Where did Blake get all these fancy clothes?

She applied simple eyeshadow and lipstick; that had always been the extent of her skills, though she figured she didn't need much more.

Standing, she gazed at Mildred, who also dressed in black. Her dress somehow flowed from her lean frame like silken mist. It hung from her left shoulder, scooping down to hook under her right arm, while preserving her modesty. The skirt covered her left leg, but her right peeked out when she walked.

She smiled. "Ready?"

"I don't know what we're heading into, so, absolutely." She wiggled her eyebrows and smiled.

Mildred smiled and hooked her arm in Tory's.

Outside their room, Sarah stood waiting for them. She stared at them. "You two look so cute together. After dinner tonight, can we hang out in the hot tub again?"

Mildred sighed. "You fell asleep in the hot tub last night. Astor and Tory ended up carrying you to the tiny loveseat and you just slept there all night instead of in your own room and your own bed. What's wrong with your room?"

The other woman slumped. "I don't know. I miss hanging out with you, that's all. It's our last night, and then you drive back down to Santa Cruz. With my job up here—two hours away, I'll remind you—we never see each other. We used to hang out all the time."

"You could come down and visit. It *is* a two hour drive, but that isn't that far. Come, visit. A weekend with us would be fun."

Sarah narrowed her eyes. "'Us' as in you and your parents or 'us' as in—" She waved her hand between Mildred and Tory. Tory's heart pounded at the idea that she and Mildred could be an 'us.'

Laughter filled the hall. "How about we talk, and figure it out as the time gets closer?"

Sarah nodded. "Fine. But I'm holding you to this."

"Good. Because I miss you, too. I forget when work gets overwhelming. I bet Andy would want to hang out with us as well."

"Oh! That would be so much fun! I'm jealous that you get to work with him." She skipped ahead of the two of them, her spirits finally turning.

Tory took a breath once the very energetic woman turned the corner ahead of them. "So much energy."

Mildred smirked as she looked down at her. "This coming from you?"

Tory just smiled.

They made it to the dining hall. It was decked out with black and wine-colored streamers and balloons. Around the sides of the room were large bouquets of flowers, interspersed with towers of bottles of wine. In the center of the room was a chocolate fountain. The tables were covered with white linen and white plates.

When they got to their seats, Tory examined the plates, running her fingers along the gold edging. The silverware wasn't silver, but gold. Each of the glasses had gold on the rims, and around the bases.

Tory and Mildred joined Mildred's parents at a round table that seated ten. With them were the full Barclay clan, which left a free seat. During most of the meal, Mildred's parents spoke business with Mr. and Mrs. Barclay. Apparently, there was a lot going on in the banking world.

Tory tried to keep track of each course—tartar, brûlée, crudité—but the plates of food were too elaborate and spectacular. After the seventh, her mind spun with flavors. Each dish was paired with a wine and by the tenth, she was surprised anyone could sit up straight.

The last dish, a small taste of tiramisu, put a smile on her face. Everything about the evening was lovely, but she was ready to be in a less formal setting.

"So, Mildred," her mother asked, "when can we expect to see you and Tory again?"

Mildred set her fork down. "I figured we'd attend the Halloween fashion show charity event."

This was news to Tory. She'd never been to a fashion show, but she liked the idea of a charity event.

Priscilla's smile widened. "That would be wonderful. I'd like us all to have matching, themed outfits. Tory, if it's acceptable, I'll have our tailor send something over to you. It's a thing, you know, being Halloween."

Tory froze, as if cold water had been splashed on her. *Are we at the matching outfit part of the relationship?* Mildred's warm hand squeezed her thigh. "We'll see, Mother. I'll let you know next week, once I explain the full extent of the event to her. No scaring off my girlfriend."

The word 'girlfriend' started rewarming Tory like a warm cup of coffee, and she smiled at Mildred, letting her know what she thought of the title.

Once the meal was done, there was a bit of schmoozing, but Mildred got them out of that as quickly as she could. They made their way to their room and locked the door. She smiled at Tory. "Okay, one more night, breakfast, and we can head back to Santa Cruz. Do you work tomorrow night?"

"No, it's the full moon. I work the rest of the week, though."

Mildred's eyes widened. "I hadn't realized that. Is it hard for you to keep track, or do you have it on your calendar?"

"I don't know. At this point it's become a habit."

They both headed towards the bedroom, then stared at each other awkwardly. It wasn't too late, but every other night, they'd had guests. Tory bit her lower lip, hope building in her gut. "So, what do you want to do?"

"We could use the hot tub again. It's nice and relaxing."

"True. And we don't have to get drunk this time."

Mildred giggled. She went into the bathroom, then sighed. "My suit is still wet. I forgot to wring it out last night."

"Well, we have a few options. You could wear a bra and panties, pretty much the same thing. Or we could go without. I won't tell if you don't."

"I think it's a bit early in our relationship, don't you?"

"Probably, so bra and undies it is."

It took Mildred a few minutes of searching through her bag, but once she found a set, she went into the bathroom to change. Tory changed in the bedroom proper once the bathroom door closed.

When the door opened, Mildred came out in a peach set that was only a few shades darker than her skin. Though in theory it was the same as a bikini, the fabric was more sheer, and Tory's breath caught. She didn't want to ruin their evening, so she forced herself to look away. "Perfect, let's get wet ... er, get into the water."

They sat on opposite sides of the tub, and as soon as Mildred's bra got wet, Tory turned away, collecting her thoughts. The cotton fabric was useless, the other woman may as well have jumped in naked.

"You okay over there, Tory? You look a bit shaken."

"I'm fine." She scooted until she sat next to Mildred. If she stayed across from her, she'd give herself away. "I know you said our relationship is new, but I really want to continue what we started up on that bridge."

Mildred's eyes widened, and Tory could smell the desire on the other woman. A smile spread on Tory's face as she realized she wasn't the only one wanting more.

Mildred's voice came out low and husky. "I'd like that too, but it's been a while for me. When it gets to be too much ..." Her voice trailed off.

Tory swung her leg over Mildred's, straddling her. She placed her hands on either side of Mildred, caging her in. Leaning down, she stole a quick kiss. "If we've hit your stopping point, we stop. If we hit my limit, we stop. This is about us enjoying each other and the escapism this room and resort weekend offers."

Before Mildred could say anything, Tory dipped her head down for another kiss, longer and deeper. Mildred gave as good as she received. She reached up and traced the lines of Tory's back, sending shivers throughout her body. Within Tory, her wolf howled its approval as she pressed her body closer.

The hot water bubbled around them as she drew her cool hand around Mildred's body, towards her taut breast. A small gasp and the tightening of her nipple preceded a low moan. Tory traced around the aureole, flicking her thumb over the most sensitive areas. Her other hand moved to twine in Mildred's hair, as she enjoyed the sounds the other woman made.

Mildred's hands, warm from being under the water, rubbed down Tory's back. When they got to her hips, one continued around her body, tracing the line of her bikini bottom. Tory groaned as a thumb slid beneath the hem and then she gasped.

It may have been a while for Mildred, but she knew what she was doing. Tory angled her hips up a bit, giving the other woman better access as she circled and teased, sending shivers of pleasure throughout her body.

Mildred pulled away from the kiss, nibbling to Tory's ear. "I want to hear you scream, Tory. I feel you trembling. Give it up for me, do it now, and we can go to that big bed and really explore with mouths and tongues."

It was too much, her body exploded. If Mildred hadn't been holding her up, she'd have fallen back into the water, and not cared. Waves of pleasure washed through her. It'd been so long since she'd been with anyone, and her body was desperate for what it had been missing. With her wolf fully onboard for this, she wanted to howl her orgasm.

Instead, she held back that little bit, as she finally came down from the desire Mildred aroused in her.

Chapter 27 - It's Like Riding a Bike
Mildred

It had been a long time since a beautiful, naked woman climbed into bed with Mildred. She'd just seen Tory orgasm in the tub, and that had been sexy as hell. She couldn't believe she'd been so bold, but something about this woman brought out her carnal nature, and she wanted more.

She'd been the one asking for them to take it slow, and now all she wanted was more. More of this woman, more touching, tasting, mindless sex. She didn't care who was doing what to whom, she wanted it all. She couldn't remember the last time she'd felt this way with another person.

As she lay on her back, Tory climbed up her body, bending to drop a kiss on her lower belly, one between her breasts, and then one on her mouth. Nothing like the scorching kiss in the hot tub, just a "hello, and welcome to act two." It somehow was just as sexy. Mildred squirmed, craving more.

Tory intertwined herself with Mildred, rubbing her thigh between Mildred's legs while gyrating herself in a slow sinuous motion. The sensation zinged through Mildred, her heart beating faster. Tory's voice flowed over Mildred, sensual and seductive. "It's my turn, and I want to hear you scream this time. Make it loud enough everyone in this resort hears us and is jealous."

Mildred took in a shaky breath and huffed out a laugh, amused at the thought. She'd never had a lot of luck with other women bringing her to orgasm. She loved being with them and always had fun, but found she did better finding a climax on her own. She didn't want to ruin the moment, so she smiled up at Tory. "Sounds good to me, sexy. Let's bring down the house."

Tory slowly kissed her way down Mildred's body. She stopped at her breasts, drawing one nipple into her mouth, her warm tongue circling the sensitive skin. Her thumb mimicked the motions on her other side. Shivers of pleasure formed heat within Mildred, her body more reactive to the petite woman than she expected.

A sucking sensation pulled at her breast, and then teeth scraped to the tip. Mildred arched up as a moan escaped her. Her head fell back as Tory continued to play.

Just as the feelings began to be too much, the other woman's wicked mouth trailed a series of kisses down her stomach. Mildred tensed, worried Tory would get frustrated when she failed to get Mildred to scream out.

Tory knelt between Mildred's legs, then slowly licked up the center of her core. When she got to the top, she hummed. "Nice."

The sound vibrated through Mildred, and she felt herself respond, her body building up in a way she wasn't used to.

Tory's mouth dropped down, her tongue slowly circling Mildred's clit, then it stroked the tip.

Mildred gasped, pushing towards the other woman, needing more.

A finger slowly slid inside her. "Hmmm, nice and slick. Your pussy is begging for more." She felt Tory put action to words. She rocked her hips in time with Tory's maneuver.

Tory's mouth returned in a quick motion, sucking hard on Mildred's clit and all Mildred's muscles tensed with desire as she groaned. Then the tongue went back to licking, circling, and flicking.

Mildred no longer knew which way was up. Her mind was a jumble of sensations.

"That's it, come for me, Mil. Don't hold back. Enjoy this."

Tory's husky voice with its demand slithered inside Mildred like her questing fingers, the final piece she needed. Her world fractured. She screamed out her orgasm as waves of pleasure took her. Her body arched as Tory continued to lick and pump with her fingers to get every bit out of her.

Finally, she collapsed on the bed, unsure if she'd ever move again. The weight of Tory curling in next to her was the last thing she remembered before sleep came.

Chapter 28 - It's My Business, so it's Pack Business
Tory

It was midafternoon when Tory made it home. When she walked into the living room with her suitcase, Orin, Connie, and Paige all looked up at her. Orin and Connie were playing cards and Paige was working on her laptop. Tory counted herself lucky that most of the rest of the pack were at work or away.

Connie smiled wide. "Welcome home, Tory. How was your weekend of fake dating?"

Tory felt her face heat as she ducked her head.

Paige whooped. "Are you telling me the 'fake' may have dropped from your dating life?"

Knowing there was no point in trying to keep anything from her family, Tory dropped her bag at the foot of the stairs, then collapsed in one of the recliner chairs with a groan. "I'm saying yes, for now. Mil and I are trying out dating."

Orin leaned forward, his eyes intent. "But she's human, right?"

Connie punched his arm. "It worked for you, didn't it? You found me when I was human." She turned to Tory. "Can I get you a mug of coffee? Orin made enough for the night, and it's freshly brewed."

"Gods, yes, please."

She leapt up and disappeared into the kitchen. Tory turned to Orin. "Yes, she's human, but right now we've only had three dates. I don't think it's anything I need to worry about."

The air practically vibrated with his ire. "You always have to worry when you're dating someone who doesn't know about us."

Paige rolled her eyes, but before she could say anything, Orin continued. "I'm not saying I disapprove. With the limited number of wolves, we don't have much choice in romantic partners. I'm just saying you can't ever be passive. Things happen. I love that you're breaking out of your 'home-work' rut. Go out, date, have a life. It's about time. But Tory, always be aware that you're dating a woman who doesn't know about us."

She sighed. "I know all this, Orin. You've been preaching this for years. Just because I left for a while doesn't mean I forgot the basics."

He leaned back in his seat. "Okay, fine. I know you're smart. I'm sorry."

Connie returned and handed her a large mug of coffee. "He only means the best, Tor, you know that. We all do."

"I know. It's just new to me. I'm not ready to be out of the fantasy stage yet."

The back door opened then closed, and Tamsin walked in. Paige leapt up and gave her a hug. "To what do I owe this? Not that I don't appreciate it."

"Oh, I'm just happy. Good news all around."

Tamsin gazed at the people in the living room, then stopped on Tory. "Something good happen up north?"

"No, well, yes. Mil and I shifted from fake to real dating." She put her hands up in the traditional stop sign and waved them. "Before you lecture me on being careful with a human, Orin already has, and I knew before he did. Don't worry."

Tamsin laughed. "I wasn't going to. I was just going to say 'good,' and 'about time.' She seems to make you happy."

The group settled down to discuss the weekend as more pack mates trickled in. Apparently, one of the heart attack victims belonged to the coven. She'd been Blake's friend who'd traveled to Santa Cruz along with her. The funeral service had been that weekend. Blake was planning on taking a bit of an extra long run to howl her emotions to the moon.

Connie leapt up. "Full moon tonight, so that's my cue to start cooking. It's an easier dinner, something quick, so I know that won't be an issue. Just to fill our bellies and get us all out running."

After her weekend at the vineyard, Tory would've been happy with cereal for dinner, but with Connie cooking, she knew it wouldn't be anything that simple. They ended up with fajitas they could build themselves. There was perfectly seasoned chicken, steak, pork, and tofu. Though the meal sounded basic, in Connie's hand and with Tamsin helping, it was a gourmet dinner.

Tory was in one of the first groups shifting, along with Connie, Orin, Maria, and Blake. The five of them ran down the path. She tried to ignore the aroma of the cats who lived near the pack house. They were the same as the previous month, as well as the dogs obsessed with them. The story she'd been creating about the interaction wasn't going to change much with the scent the animals left. It was all much the same.

Once they arrived at the meeting area, Tory caught the aroma of something new. A cougar had crossed nearby. Nose pressed to the ground, she followed the trail, sniffing deep into the grass and dirt, the earthy feline smell filling her senses. She felt two other bodies sticking near her. A deeper intake told her it was Orin and Connie.

The three of them stalked the trail she followed. It was maybe a week old, but as they went, a new trail crossed the old one. It was fresh; hours old, not days.

The three paused. Orin signaled the two to wait, then ran back to gather the rest of the pack. If they were going to go after a wild cat this big, they'd need more than the three of them.

It didn't take long for the rest of the pack to join them. Tamsin took point, and they were off. Through her magic, Tamsin orchestrated the pack, leading them as they followed the trail and then found the cougar. The fight was quick with the number of them involved and the cougar went down fast. This was their stomping ground, and they couldn't let other big predators in.

Tired from her long weekend, Tory signaled she was ready to call it a night. She did one more run to stretch her legs, her mind flashing to the vineyard and her walk with Mil. *What would it be like to run with a partner? What would it be like if Mil were a werewolf?*

She shook off the thought then headed back to pack house. She heard Blake's cry to the moon and knew not everyone would be heading home soon. This night, the pack would split, some staying out longer, running, allowing their wolves to grieve, too.

Chapter 29 - Birds of a Feather
Mildred

It had been two weeks. Mildred couldn't believe it. She sat in her office Saturday morning trying to get a few things done. She'd come in for a few minutes to get things cleaned up after a crazy week. *Two weeks. We've been dating for two weeks.* In the scheme of things, it didn't mean a lot.

Tory had to work most nights, so they had only gone out two more times, but still, it had been fantastic. Tory was amazing. Everything about this situation was ... *I have to use a different word. This can't really be this good. Something will go wrong; it always does.*

She also wanted to check in with Andy. He was working for another hour and would certainly find her.

As if on cue, a knock came to her door. "Come in."

Dennis walked in. "Can we talk about Nia?"

She smiled, biting back a laugh at her own assumptions of who was at her door. "Sure, but I'm really only here for a few minutes. Can it wait until Monday?"

"Yes, but I just want to bring it up while it's on my mind. She's been acting increasingly strange in the last six weeks. I can't put my finger on it, but if you could discretely interview the other nurses, I would appreciate it. They don't all talk to me. They may be complaining to Dwight or Tory. They seem to be the ones everyone talks to."

With a sigh, Mildred wrote down the note. Discipline was her least favorite part of the job. "I'll get this set up starting next week."

"Thanks, Mildred. Have a good weekend."

She gave him a small smile. "You, too."

Another knock broke her focus as she finished the last of what she'd come in to do. "Mil, what are you doing here?"

Looking up, she saw Andy, and her smile this time was wide and genuine. "Hoping to see you, for one. Finishing up some stuff that slipped through the cracks, for another."

He came in and fell into one of the chairs opposite her. "What can I do for you, my friend?"

"How long have you known me?"

He gave her a suspicious look. "Well, let's see. You're like a million years old."

She glared at him.

"Well, you act it. You're only thirty-two, but I swear you act twice that. Okay, we met in middle school, so twenty-some-odd years."

"Am I acting rash?" She hoped her voice didn't sound as pitiful as she felt.

"With Tory?" He leaned back and gazed up at the ceiling before looking back at her. "The woman you've been not dating and dating for weeks? You're going out like once a week, taking things slow. She's met your parents, who love her. As do Aston, Sarah, and Branson—and Branson doesn't like anyone. What exactly is rash about that?"

Mildred slumped. "I don't know. I just feel like I'm jumping into this with rose-colored glasses on. I'm only seeing good. Shouldn't I be more pragmatic, finding the bad in this as well?"

"Oh, Mil, give it time. You'll find something awful about our young Tory. Well, there's that. She's five years younger than you. A baby."

She threw a pencil at him. "If you're not going to help, then you can leave."

"Good plan. Don't you have the Halloween Gala tonight? Matching outfits. What a hoot! What's this year's theme?"

Mildred rolled her eyes. "Mother can be awful; she wanted us to all go as birds. Our outfits have feathers, a mask, and a hat. Well, I guess Tory escaped the hat." She chuckled. "Can you guess which bird Mother chose for her?"

Andy bit his bottom lip and shook his head. "Nope, not even going to go there."

Mildred huffed. "I'm going as a pelican, and Tory is a bluebird."

He barked out a laugh.

A few hours later, she and Tory were getting ready at her place. Tory had agreed to the family tailor designing her dress—a form-fitting dress with long sleeves in dark blue. The blue lightened to white as it traveled to the hem of the skirt. There were fake feathers sewn into the fabric down the body and sleeves. Her mask, which thankfully just covered her eyes, was the same blue.

Mildred wore an off-white dress with a matching mask. Her hat was a dark wine beret with a feather tuft. Both her and Tory's dresses had low-cut backs and a belt that tied in the back to represent the tail, also covered in feathers.

Tory stared at the two of them in the mirror. "This is insane. We're going to a fashion show, but we have to dress up?"

"Yep, we're there to be seen as we bask in the beauty of unrealistic fashion, then buy something that no one would ever wear."

Both Tory's brows shot up, and she chuckled. "That sounds amazing. You mean I can leave with a high-fashion outfit that can't ever be worn in public?"

"Count on it. My parents have never left without buying me, and probably by extension you, something. Make sure you decide and tell them what you like. If you don't, they'll just pick the most expensive thing there."

Her jaw dropped. "Good to know."

The venue wasn't far from Mildred's apartment. When they arrived, her mother's dress had more drape to it than the ones designed for them. It was yellow with black accents on the back, with a wide summer hat, all dripping in feathers. She smiled. "I'm an American goldfinch."

Her father wore a black tuxedo with a few red feathers on his arms and a yellow tie. He smiled wide. "Red-winged blackbird."

They sat as a group and watched the other families with their themed costumes for the evening. One group dressed as scientific elements. Another chose paranormal characters. Mildred's favorite was the group that chose winged mythological beasts: a dragon, a griffin, and a phoenix.

When the show started, the truly crazy outfits began. The designer chose an androgynous collection, dressing both men and women in similar attire. All the outfits were octopus-themed with tentacles. Some were dressed with the tentacles in waves outlining the body. One outfit was a skirt created from two tentacles woven together then warped around the waist of the man wearing it. A second woven pair encircled his chest. Each model was crazier than the last, until the final model was encased in what looked like the body of an octopus. Small protrusions around the edge of the bodice that just passed her waist represented the eight legs.

The crowd went wild as the models rewalked the runway. Mildred leaned over to Tory whose face looked ready to break from how wide her smile was. "Have you selected your favorite outfit?"

"If there's something based on that last one, a shirt with the tiny legs, that was fantastic, or the skirt and crop top made of tentacles, I'd be all over that one."

Mildred laughed. The thought of Tory in any of the outfits ... maybe a private showing, was a tantalizing thought. *This is the first year I may approve of my parents' purchases.*

As they headed back to her house, she couldn't wait to have her own fashion show.

Chapter 30 - Come Crashing Into My Life
Tory

Dennis and Dwight sat in the nurses' station, gossiping about their weekend. Tory shook her head. "When are you two going to find one person to go on more than one date with?"

Dwight snorted. "Look at you, finally dating, and now you're all judgy? I don't know if I like this new side of you."

Tory smirked. "What about that police officer? Mr. Tall, Red-Headed, and Handsome? I saw you looking at him at our last briefing."

"Him? Are you kidding? He couldn't handle all this." He waved his hand dramatically up and down to indicate his body.

Dennis snorted. "If you were all that you thought you were, *you* couldn't handle all of you. Anyway, I'm off to check room four. Have fun."

Nia walked up just as the call came in for the ambulance. They needed two. Tory stood. "I got it. Dwight, with me? Nia just got here." *Let Ms. Snaps At Everyone stay here by herself. She'll get in less trouble.*

They ran off to meet the truck.

The EMT gave the rundown. "Car crash. Driver dead on arrival, as was her passenger. The other driver sustained injuries but is alive. Condition stable."

Tory escorted the two dead patients to the morgue while Dwight took the very alive and lively one to a room to start checking her in.

The forensic pathologist had gotten the digital report on the two patients. She collected them from

Tory, who asked, "Hey, Sheryl, can you let me know the cause of death for the driver? I read over the notes on the elevator ride down. She seemed to have been healthy. This is odd."

"Sure thing. I hear you're collecting odd cases."

"Thanks!"

Back at the nurses' station, Nia smiled at Tory. "I hear you're dating Mildred. Are you trying to save your job?"

"What do you mean, save my job?"

"I hear you've been reported a few times for errors. I just figured, since you're probably on probation at this point, you're trying to sleep with the boss to save your job."

Tory stared at the woman who sat there, playing with her stupid leather boots. The damn footwear were the least practical things to wear, but the woman herself was impractical, so why not?

"I don't know where you're getting your gossip, Nia, but you need to find a better source. For your information, I'm good at my job. As for who I date, maybe if you focused on your own life, you wouldn't have such a hard time finding someone who wanted to date you. Now, if you'll excuse me, I need to go check on a patient in room three."

She spun on her heel and walked away. As she walked, she unclenched her jaw and fists before anyone noticed how angry the other nurse made her.

"Bitch," Nia mumbled low, under her breath. Tory wanted to call her out, but the only reason she'd heard was her superhuman hearing.

Turning the corner, she ran into Dennis. "It's about time you put her in her place. She's been snapping at you since you started. I don't know what she has against you, but it's bad."

"I don't know either, but I figured if I kept my distance, then she'd leave me alone."

He scoffed. "It's not in her nature. Until you're fired, I doubt she'll do any 'leaving you alone.'"

Tory slumped. "Well, I don't know what to do. It isn't like the departments are that big. I can't avoid her. We will always end up on shifts together."

"You're not wrong. I try to separate the two of you, but you're both night nurses most of the time."

"I'll just go get a cheese bagel from the cafeteria and hope she's with a patient when I return."

Dennis smiled. "Grab two, and maybe a couple of coffees. Tonight already feels like a long night, and we've barely begun."

Chapter 31 - Date Night
Mildred

It had been a month. Mildred climbed in her car. They'd been dating for a month, and it had been ... perfect. She started it and headed towards Tory's place. Well, not perfect, but really good. After the third or fourth date, Mildred had always broken it off with other women because things just didn't work out. But Tory was different—smart, tender, honest. They hadn't been on many dates, but tonight they were going out for a casual dinner and back to her place.

How many people get excited about a casual date? I need to get my life evaluated.

They'd decided to go for Chinese food. Tory requested a place where jeans and a T-shirt would be acceptable. She was tired of dressing up. "I'm running out of clothes I can borrow from my friends."

She drove up to the swank commune where Tory lived. Situated in a prime location, the sprawling blue building always impressed her. Tory stood out front in tight, black jeans and a white T-shirt with an octopus on it. In each of the eight arms, it held a mug of coffee. Across the top, it stated, *This may be enough, but you should still be wary in your approach.*

Mildred chuckled as Tory got in the car. "Where did you find that shirt?"

"Isn't it great? I thought after the Halloween event, I had to get something thematic. If I'm ever allowed to wear a T-shirt in front of your parents, this baby's coming out again. Trust me."

"My parents will laugh." She pulled out and headed towards the restaurant. "Speaking of them,

I know you mentioned Thanksgiving with your friends and family was really important. What about the Saturday afterward? Mother was hoping you'd join us for a family dinner."

Tory leaned back and gave Mildred a broad smile that warmed her to her toes. "I'd love to. I'll see about swapping with someone for the day."

"Excellent. I'll let Mother know. She'll be thrilled."

Mildred parked and they headed into the restaurant. The hostess seated them by the window and handed out menus. After a few minutes, Tory put hers down. "This becomes an important question. It could shake our relationship to its core. Do you eat Chinese food individually, or family style?"

Mildred leaned back and considered. She tilted her head and stared at the other woman. "That *is* a very important question. I've heard about countries going to war over how meals should be eaten in such places as this."

"Facts."

Nodding, Mildred put her own menu down. "Well, in my humble opinion, with the large platters of food served, and the excellent variety of offerings, it would be a shame to do anything other than family style."

Tory gave her a smile that melted her heart. "Excellent. Then we should decide what we both like to eat. The second thing that brings families to their knees."

"True, true. I like shrimp fried rice, Mongolian beef, or beef with pea pods."

"Okay," Tory said, brow furrowed in thought. "I like pork fried rice, General Tso's chicken, and mu shu Pork."

Before they could continue their discussion, the waitress came. Mildred smiled and ordered everything they both liked. Tory laughed. "You know, I can eat a lot, but that's even beyond me."

"Ah, but who doesn't like leftovers?"

"Oh, that's a good counterpoint. You know, the waitress looked scandalized."

Mildred leaned over and kissed Tory. "I don't care."

After dinner, they made their way back to Mildred's place. They hadn't ever gone back to Tory's. She said it was a madhouse, and Mildred's offered more privacy. For the most part, Mildred didn't mind. She figured it'd only been a month, and she'd make it over there eventually.

Once they'd put the food away, Mildred leaned in and kissed Tory, heat sizzling down to her toes. They continued to kiss, stripping off layers of clothes until they got to the bedroom. Mildred tenderly ran her fingers down Tory's soft back, wanting to touch every inch of her. Tory gripped Mildred's ass, tugging her in so their bodies rubbed together.

Pulling away from the kiss, Mildred said, her voice rough with need, "I want to lick you ... everywhere."

Tory groaned as Mildred pushed her onto the bed.

She scooted back, and Mildred grabbed her foot, sucking and nibbling on her toe, slowly kissing her way up Tory's long, toned leg. When she reached Tory's inner thigh, she placed the foot down on the bed and started in on the other leg. Tory squirmed. Mildred chuckled. "Be patient. I said every inch, and I meant it."

Mildred dragged her teeth and tongue up Tory's inner thigh. The other woman's muscles convulsed under her as she tried to move her body. Switching sides, Mildred said, "If you don't behave, I'll have to start all over."

Tory moaned. "You're killing me."

Mildred laughed. "Let me enjoy my dessert."

As she licked closer to the junction of Tory's legs, she slowly eased a finger inside her. She was dripping wet. Tory arched up, practically panting with need.

"You like that, don't you?"

"Gods, yes."

Mildred used two fingers and continued to slowly stroke inside as she kissed ever so slowly down her thigh. The heat within her growing.

When she got to the top of Tory's long legs, she looked up into the light blue eyes and licked off one, then the other finger. "You taste amazing."

Tory quivered, her breath choppy.

Then Mildred smiled. Slid her fingers back in and dipped her head down to feast. A groan escaped her as she spun her tongue around Tory's clit, flicking, and sucking. Then she licked down and up the center of her core. With her other hand, she reached up to play with Tory's breast.

It took a few minutes, but Tory broke, screaming, "Mil, oh, gods! Mil!" Her taut body practically levitated before collapsing.

Mildred continued to kiss her way up the other woman's body until she reached her mouth. Tory kissed her back. "Your turn."

"Not tonight. Tomorrow. For now, enjoy your pleasure."

Tory curled into her. Mildred wrapped her arms around her and imagined having this every night.

Where did that thought come from? We've only been together for a month!

Chapter 32 - The Wool Ripped Away ...
Tory

Tory had expected Thanksgiving with Mildred's family to be an uptight, somber affair. Fancy clothes, fancy plates, and silverware she barely understood—start from the outside and work your way in, Connie had explained—and food that left her aching for something familiar. What she hadn't expected was a party.

The family had invited all the staff to join them. Apparently, they always celebrated on Saturday to ensure everyone who worked for them had Thursday off, but then they could come and have a second meal with them, bringing their family along. Kids of all ages ran around, and some grandparents rolled around in wheelchairs.

I could be with the pack with this level of noise and joy. It's fantastic. Maybe someday Mil can join the pack for our celebration. A sense of reality and the potential complications of their relationship hit her. *Not now, Tory. Just enjoy the day.*

The family erected a tent in the backyard to accommodate the large number of people. Underneath were tables groaning under the weight of turkey, ham, potatoes—three kinds!—yams, Brussel's sprouts, baked greens, corn, mac and cheese, salad, rolls, and even more tables with selections of pies. In the center of it all was a giant chocolate fountain. Unlike at the resort weeks before, there were long skewers that people—kids and adults alike—could fill with items like fruit or marshmallows to dip into the flow.

This is fantastic. These people are amazing.

Tory smiled at Mildred. "You didn't warn me. It's perfect."

"I'm glad you love this as much as I do."

"Your family does this every year?"

Mildred wrapped her arm around Tory's shoulders. "For as long as I can remember. This has always been my favorite day of the year. I love getting gifts on Christmas, and on Thanksgiving proper we have a nice day. We usually go out and volunteer at a soup kitchen. Still, today, the Saturday afterward, when we can celebrate with all the people around us ... I just love it."

Just after noon, they sat, plates filled with food, and dug in. Everything tasted amazing. As always, the food the pack had made was delicious, but so was this. She couldn't believe how well she was eating ... again!

Her phone buzzed. She wanted to ignore it, but she checked the display and saw it was Bexlee. She raised her eyebrows. Bexlee never called her. She was a police officer heading up the case that ran parallel to the heart attack victims Tory had been tracking all fall, which had begun as pulmonary embolism victims. When she'd told Bexlee her theory, the other wolf was the only one who'd believed her.

Tory could only think of one reason for her packmate to call her. They'd talked about her event. If Tory remembered correctly, Bexlee had a date with her girlfriend, and they were going to go hang out with Officer Ezra. The only reason for the call would be case-related.

Her heart started pounding harder in her chest. *This can't be good. Did someone we both know get hurt? Is another witch dead? Or worse, a wolf?*

"Mil, this is important. I need to take it."

Laughing with one of the kids, Mildred smiled and nodded at her.

Tory stood, answering the phone as she walked away. "Bexlee, what's up?"

"Tory, I may need your help. It's Cyrus, um, Officer Ezra. He was poisoned with the heart attack concoction."

"Oh, my gods! Tell me everything. Have you spoken to Tamsin?"

"She's next. I just, can you get here ... just in case?"

She took a calming breath. "Of course. Text the address. I'm on my way."

Sliding the phone into her purse, Tory put on her nurse's face. She quickly walked back to Mildred. "I'm so, so, so sorry. It's an emergency. Could I possibly take your car?"

Mildred's eyes snapped to hers. "Is everything okay?" She shook her head. "Of course, it isn't. Do you want me to come with you?"

Tory bit her lip. "But ... this is your day, your family's day."

Her warm hands clasped Tory's and squeezed. "If you need me, then you are my priority. I'll just go explain it to Mother and Father. They'll be disappointed, but they'll understand. Family is important." As worried as she was, a part of Tory melted at the word 'family.'

It took a few minutes, but they were soon on their way. Tory gave Mildred a skeleton explanation of what had happened.

"So, wait, Officer Court lives in that monstrosity of a building with you, and you know her?"

"Yes. She and I grew up together."

Mildred's head bobbed slowly as she drove. "Did you know Officer Ezra before that first meeting as well?"

Tory huffed out a laugh. Her mind was preoccupied with what they may find in that backyard. Would they be too late? Would the nice officer be dead? Would Bexlee have to find a new partner? "No. That was the first time I'd met him. Actually, I've only seen him in those meetings."

"Got it. And the police have found a ... concoction that is causing these odd heart attacks, and Bexlee thinks this material got into something he ate or drank?"

She nodded, then realized Mildred may not see it, since she drove the car. "Yes, and no. I don't know why she didn't call for an ambulance. We can ask when we get there."

Bexlee's text provided an address and directions to come through the unlocked front door and straight to the backyard. Tory recognized Bexlee's car, so she knew they had the right place. They got out and ran.

They burst through the back door to find Bexlee and Officer Ezra sitting in a couple of chairs, talking. Irritation flashed within Tory. "What! I thought—"

Bexlee's head jerked to theirs, eyes wide. "Tory, oh, my gods, I forgot to text you back. We got it figured out."

Ire turned to frustration. "What happened? Was it a false alarm? He looks fine. You look fine. Everyone looks hale and healthy here."

Officer Ezra shot to his feet with a wide smile. "The nurse! Are you also a werewolf?"

Tory's world dropped from under her. She gaped at the tall officer, then at Bexlee, and finally she turned to Mildred, who'd stopped behind her.

Mildred hadn't been listening to them. She'd been transfixed by something to their left in the yard. Turning slowly, ice cold chills of terror shot through her body as she watched Wynn, Bexlee's girlfriend, complete her shift from wolf to human.

Chapter 33 - It's an Omission, Not a Lie
Mildred

Mildred watched in horror and fascination. The thing ... the thing ... had been a wolf. Her mind screamed; there was no way. When she and Tory entered the officer's backyard, to their left there had been an animal—a dog? a wolf?—stretching, back arched. But then the stretching didn't stop. It's body started to bulge in ways that her mind didn't understand, but whatever was happening had a beauty to it.

And then, the hair began to recede. Mildred shut her eyes, trembling, shaking her head. *I know I saw a gray wolf when I walked back here, but now ... is that a woman? A naked woman emerging from the animal? A beautiful, naked woman?*

When she reopened her eyes, the woman breathed hard, perched on her hands and knees, a wash of wavy, light brown hair hiding her face.

Tory appeared in front of her. "Mil. Hey, Mil. Look at me, focus on me."

Her girlfriend's clear blue eyes were the size of saucers. She didn't look freaked out, she looked ... worried. "Tory? Are you upset? Did you see that? I thought I saw a wolf ... but there's a naked woman there now ... and am I losing my mind?" Mildred bounced her eyes back and forth between the fully-formed woman in the yard and Tory.

Officer Court brought the other woman clothes. She kept shooting Mildred and Tory looks over her shoulder. She looked uncertain as well.

Why isn't anyone else freaked out?

"I'm not upset, I'm just worried about you and what you saw." Tory words centered Mildred. She clung to them. Tory seemed to be the only real thing in the backyard.

"Me? I'm fine." Her voice didn't sound like her, and she felt like she was under water, drowning. Nothing was real. "But, Tory, what did I see? Do you know what I saw?" *How could she know? She and I arrived together. Why isn't she freaking out?* Mildred's breath started to come out rough. *I can't breathe.*

From her right, Officer Ezra laughed. "There be wolves in my backyard. Everyone here is a wolf. Fe Fi Fo Fum! I smell a wolf in human skin!"

Officer Court turned from the woman—the wolf?—who had slipped into the clothes and sighed. "Cyrus, do you know how to keep your mouth shut? Why not fill another plate and eat? Tamsin is on her way over. She'll explain things to you, get you integrated—" her eyes drifted to Mildred, "—to where you understand things. Until then, can you just let us clean up this mess?"

The woman ... wolf? Snorted. "Why did you bring a vanilla here, Tory? Great planning."

"Fuck you, Wynn. I was called and told to hurry. I came. See if I help you next time."

Cyrus threw his head back and laughed. "Now it's a cat fight!"

Does one of them become a cat? What the fuck crazy-ass backyard has Tory brought me into? What are they going to do to me? Mildred stepped back, wrapping her arms around herself.

Bexlee snarled. "Just stop! Both of you. This situation is bad enough, we don't need you two making it worse." The officer shot a glance at Mildred. "If we could all just take it down a level, maybe we can clear the air of some of our ... jokes?"

She's editing what she's saying. What doesn't she want me to know? 'Jokes.' Does she think I'm an idiot? Am I an idiot? They're all lying by omission. It isn't just Tory. What's going on here?

Mildred turned from the stranger who'd finally stood and searched for the mess Officer Court described. Everything in the backyard looked pretty neat to her. A table of food, a few chairs ... she wondered what mess this Tamsin person was needed for. *Is she another cop?*

Tory's hands slid up to Mildred's cheeks. "Sweetie, can we talk?"

She focused on the other woman. "Isn't that what we're doing?"

"No, you keep spacing out. Can you tell me what you're thinking? What you saw?"

Mildred opened up her mouth, then shut it. How could she say what she saw? The beautiful stranger came over to them. "She saw me shift." She sighed and the fight seemed to melt from her. "I'm sorry. Tory, I didn't know you two were coming, otherwise, I'd have waited. Hidden until you two left."

A pit opened under Mildred, and her gut clenched. The reality of the situation crashed down on her. *Tory really does know what's going on. Is an omission a lie?* "This can't be real. Did you slip a drug to me?" Her voice came out low and breathy.

Tory's hands rubbed down her arms. "No, this isn't a hallucination. We aren't lying to you or playing tricks. It's a part of my world ... the part I'm not allowed to share, not without permission."

"Without permission? What do you mean, 'permission?'" Mildred's voice started to rise. "Wait, what do you mean 'your world?' Are you saying you think people can turn into wolves? That was a wolf, right? That's what the officer was saying. He said you're all wolves? Is there more than one wolf out here?"

"Yes, that's what he said. Me, Bexlee, and Wynn. We're all werewolves."

Bexlee sighed. "And Cyrus."

Tory's head snapped to her. "What?"

"It's a long story. The moral is, the concoction doesn't work on us, and I didn't want him to die."

Tory eyes widened as her jaw clenched at the new information. Then she shook her head. "Shit. I mean, I'm glad he's alive, but shit. Wynn?"

Bexlee shook her head. "No, I did it. But he's still reeling." She waved at Officer Ezra, who was grinning. "As you can see."

Mildred wanted to laugh. "So, you all believe werewolves are real." She shut her eyes and took a deep breath. *The drinks must've been really strong at the party today, that's all. I'm drunk. I'll wake up with a killer headache and everything will be back to the way it was.* "Tory, can we talk ... away from everyone else?"

"Use the house. We'll be out here." Officer Ezra waved at them then sat back and took a swig of his beer.

Tory led Mildred into the house, and they found a couch to sit on. Mildred took a deep breath. "Look, one of my favorite things about you, besides you being funny and smart, is the honesty we've shared. All of a sudden there's a whole side of you, and I mean something huge, that you've lied to me about. I don't know how I feel about that."

"It isn't that I've lied, I just haven't told you about this one thing. It's safer."

"Safer for who?"

Tory slumped. "Everyone. There aren't many werewolves in the world. We keep our secret well-guarded. The only people who know about us are other wolves and our mates, um, spouses. If we had gotten to that point, I would've opened up to you, but it isn't something we talk about otherwise."

"I get it on a logical level." And she did. Mildred wasn't sure she'd have made a different decision in Tory's place. "But on an emotional one, I feel betrayed. I don't know how I feel about my girlfriend keeping this from me for all these weeks. You don't trust me."

Tory's religion suddenly occurred to her, and she laughed. "Artemis. You worship the full moon. God above, that was slick. You're good." She wanted to kick herself for her idiocy.

"Please, Mil, listen to me. I do trust—"

"No!" she yelled. "No, I don't think you do, and I don't think I'll listen. You've had weeks to tell me about this, and you didn't. I don't know that I want to hear about it now." She stood. "I assume if I head back to my parents to enjoy what's left of my ruined day, you can find your own way home?"

"Mil, please." Tears fell from Tory's eyes. Mildred slowed, but then pushed the feelings away. Tory had made a choice, and that was that. "I don't want to lose you. I ... I ... gods, please. I—"

"Don't say it. You have no right to say that." She pointed her finger at Tory, glaring all her wrath, hoping Tory could feel some of her hurt. "I'm going to walk out that door and you will *not* follow. The next time I see you I'm your boss at work and you're my employee."

"You're breaking up with me?"

Mildred felt her heart breaking. "You lied to me." She got up and walked out the front door. She wished the shutting of the door would shut her emotions away as easily as it hid Tory from her.

Chapter 34 - Meeting of the Minds
Tamsin

Tamsin pulled up to the address Bexlee had texted her. There were a few cars already there, but she found a spot. Her phone had buzzed on the drive over, so she checked her texts as soon as she parked.

"Shit!" Bexlee had sent a message that Mildred had seen Wynn shift and didn't seem happy. She worried about the fallout.

This is bad but not the end of the world. It's all about communication and de-escalation.

With a sigh, she got out of the car. As she shut her door, the front door opened and a tall, well-put-together woman came out. *That must be Mildred. I hope this turns out well for Tory, she deserves the best. Here's hoping for the best.*

She walked up to the woman. "Hi. Mildred?"

"Do I know you?" Mildred snapped. Tamsin could feel the fear, anger, and sadness rolling off of her.

"My name's Tamsin. I was hoping we could speak."

Her eyes narrowed as she sneered, "Are you one of them? A cop? Or some other type of leader? They said you were coming over to clean up the mess."

"You could say I'm a leader. I was hoping you and I could talk—just for a minute or two."

"I can't imagine what you'd say that would change anything." She crossed her arms across her chest and glared. "Do werewolves kill humans who find out about them? Is that why you're here? Is that why they let me leave? Are you the clean-up crew?"

Tamsin sighed. "No, we don't just kill people. We ask that you help to keep our secret. If you go around telling people, no one's going to believe you anyway. It really isn't something we worry too much about, to be honest."

"Are you dangerous?"

"As dangerous as any other human. We *are* stronger and faster than the average human, so when a wolf goes bad, we deal with our own. But for the most part, the fear of exposure is enough."

Mildred's eyes narrowed. "She lied to me. I take trust very seriously."

"And I don't blame you. I just ask that you think about it. Don't write her off just yet."

The other woman's dark eyes searched the top of the trees. "If she has all of you, why does she even need me?"

Tamsin offered a small smile. "I wanted to speak with you about that and thank you. I grew up with Tory, and I haven't seen her happier in years. She's been lost in her work, ignoring anything else. Before work, it was school. You've gotten her out of her shell, and it's been amazing to see."

"I know it was just an omission, but it feels like a lie. I just don't know if I can get past that."

Tamsin made a sound of agreement. "If it helps, she kept this from you because it's one of our rules, like, the first rule. If it got out that werewolves were real and people believed it and that they could be changed into wolves, we'd be hunted to extinction, or studied, or worse. Right now, we live our lives and that's how we like it."

The other woman's eyes widened. "Could she have changed me into a werewolf? Am I going to grow fangs and claws?"

Tamsin chuckled. "No. It takes a serious bite to do that. And we prefer the person to request to be turned. If you don't want to become a wolf, then it won't happen."

"Wait, if I want it ..." She let the sentence hang.

"Why don't you think about everything you've seen and heard, then talk with Tory? She really cares for you."

The other woman looked shocked as she made her way to the car.

I hope I helped. I can feel how devastated Tory is.

As she passed through the house to the backyard she saw her packmate, her friend, sitting on a couch, gazing into nothing. Tears rolled down her face.

"Do you want to talk?"

Tory trembled. "No. Maybe later. Or never."

Tamsin hesitated, but sensed her need for solitude. It hurt to wrench herself away from someone in pain, but she would hear Tory's words, listen to her needs, and act accordingly.

It felt like each door of this house was a portal. Confusion and defiance out front. Pain and loss inside. And the backyard? Here Tamsin found concern, but also a party.

Bexlee, Wynn, and Cyrus all sat around a small table eating food and drinking beer. *Gods, I need a beer!* Tamsin grabbed a bottle and joined them.

Cyrus smiled and raised his bottle. "Welcome to my home, 'oh, fearless leader.'"

Oh! He'll be fun.

After the tension of the last few minutes, Tamsin sank into her seat, lifted her bottle, and relaxed. "Thanks."

Wynn darted a look at the house. "How is Tory?"

Tamsin shook her head then sipped her beer. "Not good, but she needs space. Let's focus on you." She tilted the end of her bottle at Cyrus.

He made a wide-eyed, shocked face, lifting his hand to his chest with a gasp. "Me?"

"We don't like bringing people over to our side without a lot of talk and information first. I let

Bexlee use her best judgment with you, and I'm sorry if it was the wrong decision."

"Hell no. I mean, I have no idea what all this means, but alive and knowing more? And werewolves are real?" He lifted his drink in cheer. "Fuck, yeah!"

Bexlee and Wynn chuckled. Tamsin smiled. "Good. Over the next few months, you'll learn a lot. Here are a few basics. Most of us prefer being part of a pack, though it's not mandatory. Wynn can tell you about the life of a lone wolf."

Next to her, Wynn snorted. "Weren't you a lone wolf for, like, five years in Chicago?"

"Well, yes. Okay, either of us can. I would suggest starting off as part of the pack until you figure things out."

His brow knit. "It's not a demand?"

Bexlee sighed and rolled her eyes. "You're an adult, Cyrus. You can make up your own mind"

"Right, sure, okay." He didn't sound convinced.

Tamsin sipped her beer. "I'd like you to meet the pack, run with us at the next full moon, and learn about what you've become. I think lessons on your new superpowers are extremely important."

"My what now?"

"As a werewolf, all your senses are enhanced to some degree. We'll need to work with you to test them out. Sight, smell, hearing, stamina, strength, lie detection. Everything. You're going to be overwhelmed. Keep Bex in the loop at work. Get away from groups when it gets to be too much. And this," she wiggled her bottle, "won't do what it used to do."

He groaned at that. Then he froze, his face draining of color. "Does the pack shift together? Do that 'getting naked thing' before becoming a wolf?"

Bexlee seemed to understand his issue. "Don't worry, no one in the pack will care. And if you want to shift alone, Tamsin will arrange for that. We shift in stages. She should know. No one else has to."

Tamsin tilted her head. "Strange scar? Injury from the job?"

Cyrus snarled. "No." Then he sighed. "I was assigned female at birth."

He gazed at Tamsin as if waiting for something.

She waited for something else. Something big and earth-shattering. When that was all he had to say, she nodded. "Okay. I'm betting you'll have a male wolf; our inner beasts are smarter than us. So, no one has to know. You'll shift in my group, along with Bex and Wynn. You can let the others know if and when you want to and are ready to do so. Just so you know, no one will see you as anything other than as you are." She smiled warmly. "Be welcome in my pack, Cyrus."

Chapter 35 - A Chance Comment Can Mean the World
Tory

Monday evening, Tory lost herself in her work. She tried to avoid the nurse's station, spending her time checking on patients, making sure everything was stocked, and hiding out at a solitary computer station when she could.

She didn't see Mildred during their few hours of overlap. If she visited the emergency department—not unusual—Tory had been off in her own world, occupied.

She knew she'd hurt Mildred by keeping secrets, but there hadn't been any other way. Now she felt torn, like her soul had been ripped asunder. She'd been in relationships before that had ended, but none hurt like this. Someone had scooped out her guts and replaced them with lead. They'd used her chest as a punching bag and left her broken but not dead. Sometimes she thought death would be a blessing. She had no more tears—or so she hoped, running around work. That was the last thing she needed.

Well past the time Mildred would be gone, and tired beyond reason—emotions were draining—she gave in and dropped onto one of the nurses' station chairs. Dwight was the only one there, and she could usually count on him for some outlandish story about his weekend.

Instead of gossiping, he looked her up and down. "I wasn't even sure you were here tonight. The blue flashes of your hair were the only indications you were working. What are you running from, woman?"

Nia walked up. "Working too hard if you ask me." She looked and sounded ... friendly. Nothing good could come from this "You look dead on your feet, Tory. I just got a bottle of water from the vending machine. Looks like you need it more than me. Want it?"

Tired as she was, Nia being pleasant still raised her hackles. On the other hand, her pounding head told her she was dehydrated. She lifted her hand and nodded in thanks. The old leather scent of Nia's boots tickled her nose, and she sneezed—she was too tired to hold it back.

Nia's brow rose. "If you're sick, then you should go home. No need to make our patients worse." She sounded condescending as she said it. And there it was!

"I'm fine, just the flowers over there." She waved vaguely towards one of the rooms. "I have allergies," she lied.

"Ay! You never bring me water!" Dwight complained, obviously changing the subject. "What? Am I chopped liver?"

Nia rolled her eyes, but Dennis arrived before she could answer. "Don't any of you work? Y'all just sitting here gossiping and complaining! New patient in the waiting room."

Dwight leapt up. "On it, boss."

Tory watched as Nia slunk off towards the solitary computer, the spot she'd hid in earlier. As Nia walked away, she heard a squeak. Scanning down, she noticed the other woman wore practical sneakers tonight. *Why does she smell like leather? Maybe I'm just expecting it at this point, or I'm way too tired to be here tonight.*

With a sigh, she slipped off to her locker and put the water bottle in her bag. For some reason, she just didn't trust it. *I'm not trusting anything from that bitch, no matter how nice she pretended to be tonight.*

She went and bought a new one and drank deeply. She debated a second bottle.

Passing Nia, she lifted the nearly empty water bottle in salute. Nia smirked back with a small wave. Shaking her head, Tory ignored Nia and returned to her patients.

The next morning, when she got home, Bexlee was in the kitchen, pouring coffee, about to leave for work. "Isn't this late for you to leave?"

"Normally, yes. Cyrus and I requested a later start. His daily training begins tomorrow, six to seven, and then we'll head to work. Orin agreed to help."

"That's fantastic. Sorry to barge in on Saturday."

Bexlee's eyes softened. "No, I'm sorry. I should've sent a text to follow up. I should've thought. It was a horrible comedy of errors."

Tory shook her head. "Look, I'm falling over on my feet. Someone gave me a bottle of water today. I don't know why I distrust her, but I do. Can you maybe have your lab run tests on it?"

"Whoa, you think it's tainted?"

"I do."

"Then you've found a black witch?"

"And maybe their scent marker."

Chapter 36 - A Fox in the Hen House
Mildred

Mildred trudged to her car, heading to work. It had been five days since she'd broken up with Tory and she wasn't any closer to figuring things out. Her heart ached for the other woman. She'd never hurt for anyone after a breakup as much as she did with Tory. *But she lied to me! How can I trust her if she lied to me? But ... would I do any differently in her place? She was protecting herself. Not only herself, her family.*

She'd been going round and round on this for days. Never getting any closer. At work, she'd done her job, including monitoring the emergency room. In each of her trips down, she hadn't run into Tory. In her updates, Dennis had given her run-downs of every member of the crew, including Tory, but she hadn't actually seen the blue-haired wonder.

She parked and entered the hospital. After getting her regular coffee and muffin, she made it to her office without seeing anyone who needed her immediate attention. She knew she had some time this morning to get work done. No meeting, no rounds, no responsibilities. She couldn't often finagle a day like this, but when she could, she enjoyed the gift.

She put down her coffee and began to organize.

An hour later, she'd made some real progress. Not having interruptions gave her time to dig in and actually accomplish things. The loud clatter of her phone rattled her, and she leapt nearly a foot off her chair. "For fuck's sake, who's calling me?" *I should have another hour at least before I get any interruptions. Not even Andy has come around.*

She picked up the phone and grumbled, "Doctor Quincy, how can I help you?"

"Mil? It's Brandy. Perfect. I'm glad you're in your office. The police called ... an Officer Ezra? Anyway, they have some new information and want us to meet them in an hour. They were hoping the two nurses from the emergency room could join us. Tory and Dwight. I was hoping you could get that all arranged."

Mildred's jaw clenched, and for a moment she wasn't sure she could speak. Making herself breath, she nodded, then dragged the words out, forcing her voice to be chipper. "We'll be there."

"Excellent. One hour, in the conference room."

She hung up and her stomach did a backflip. Not only did she have to see Tory, she had to find her and speak with her. Arrange a meeting with her. Socialize. Her hand began to tremble. Mildred yearned to be in the same room with Tory, touch her, hold her, kiss her. It'd been almost a week, and her body craved the other woman. It was only her logical mind that kept her from running to Tory and begging her to take her back.

She lied to me. She didn't trust me. If she can keep being a werewolf a secret, then what else isn't she telling me that's important? Can I trust her?

Sniffling, Mildred grabbed a tissue and tried to pull herself together. After a few shaky breaths, she felt ready to take the next step. She picked up the phone and called the emergency department.

"Dennis speaking."

"Hi, Dennis, it's Mildred. There's another meeting with the police. It's scheduled to start in an hour. I don't know what this one will be about, but they've requested both Tory and Dwight."

"Huh. They're both on tonight. I'll give them a call and see if they can get in early. I'll call up to Dr. Tells to approve their overtime."

"Sounds good. Thanks."

She hung up, then leaned back for a moment to let her body decompress before she could focus on work for the last few minutes before the meeting.

When she walked into the meeting, Tory and Dwight were already there. Like last time, Dr. Tells sat at the head of the table with Brandy on one side and Dwight on his other. Tory sat beside Dwight. Before Mildred could take her seat, Brandy swung around in her chair and smiled up at Mildred.

"Why don't you go sit next to Dwight and Tory? We'll present a united front."

Robotically, Mildred nodded and walked around the table. A minute or two later, Officer Court and Officer Ezra joined them. Officer Ezra smiled at everyone, his expression a bit manic. "Well, hello. I'd like to introduce each of you to my new partner, Officer Court. My former partner left the force. Officer Court is an excellent replacement, and we are lucky to have her."

Mildred saw Tory try to suppress a smile, the twinkle in her eye unmistakable. She looked around, wondering if she should mention that she'd met both officers outside of the hospital ... *does it matter?*

Officer Court sat on the edge of her seat. "To be honest, I know Nurse Byrd. We grew up together. I don't want you to find out later and feel like either of us hid anything from you. On Monday, she was handed a bottle of water under what she felt was suspicious circumstances."

On Tory's other side, Dwight perked up. "Are you talking about Nia? That was strange. That woman would watch a person die of dehydration before she shared shit with them. Pardon my French."

Officer Court huffed out a laugh. "Anyway. I had the bottle tested, and the concoction that causes the heart attacks in people was in that bottle. There was a pinprick hole in the cap where it must have been administered."

Doctor Tells's eyes widened. "Are you saying one of our nurses tried to poison someone?"

"Yes." Officer Court said. "We sent some officers to pick her up. We hope it'll be enough to get to the bottom of this mess. We still need to figure out who's putting the concoction out there. Our goal here was to follow up and to thank you all for staying vigilant."

Mildred thought about the concoction. It had led to Officer Ezra becoming a werewolf ... and her breakup with Tory. "Has a counteragent or cure been able to be manufactured from any of the survivors?"

"No. It's a long story, and if you want to talk about this, we can, but unfortunately, there isn't time now. Officer Ezra and I need to get back to the precinct."

After that, it didn't take long for the meeting to break up. Mildred wanted to ask Tory if she knew more about the cure than the officers were stating, but when she looked for her, only Dwight remained in the room.

He shrugged. "She's been avoiding colleagues all week. Her work with patients has been great, but the woman's been a ghost. Any ideas why?"

She just shook her head and went searching.

Chapter 37 - A Decision Made
Tory

Once the meeting ended, Tory slipped away. She wanted to talk with Bexlee and Cyrus, but not enough to chance speaking with Mil ... Mildred, she lost the right to her boss's nickname. She'd avoided the other woman for most of the week, and she figured if she could make it until next week, her emotions would be under control.

In all her life, she'd never been this controlled by the damn things, and Tory wouldn't let them continue to dictate her state of mind now.

But, Tory, when a wolf picks a mate, you can't help but be more connected to the other person.

She wanted to squash her inner voice. Mildred wasn't her mate. Her mate, when she found that magical person, wouldn't squash her into a mess of emotions like this.

When she got down two floors, she debated where to go. She didn't have to check into the emergency department for another few hours. They'd offered her extra pay for the meeting, but she was pretty sure that was *only* for the meeting.

Food. I'll head to the cafeteria, get food, then either read a book or watch a movie on my phone. That should use up my time nicely.

She changed course. The cafeteria had surprisingly decent food. It wasn't spectacular, but it wasn't awful. She filled her tray with a curry over rice and a side salad. There were brownies and they looked too good to pass up. Add to that a mug of coffee and a bottle of water—untainted— and she thought she'd be good. For a few minutes at least.

There was a table in the corner under a window. Sunlight washed over the area, warming it. She tucked in, mostly hidden from the other people in the room, and sighed. She was rarely alone, and it felt nice.

The curry was bland, but not horrible. She took out her phone and ended up deciding to read. She lost herself in a book about a boy living on another planet who befriended a girl from their world. A portal let them talk. She loved high fantasy, and this book, *Wyldling Snare*, was lovely.

The clatter of a tray landing on her table pulled her from a dream sequence where the boy flew. She looked up into the dark eyes of Mildred Quincy, her boss, and the mistress of her emotions.

She slowly put down her spoon and phone. "Mil ... um, Mildred. I didn't expect to see you here." Her heart fluttered, but she forced her face to stay neutral. *She's so beautiful. Gah! Stop it!*

"May I join you?"

Tory swallowed, her dry throat betraying her. She lifted her coffee mug, but it was empty. Thankfully, the water bottle—her last resort—was full. She took a sip and nodded. "Of course. Always."

A small smile tugged on the side of Mildred's mouth as she sat. "It's been almost a week. I want to talk. You're a hard one to find when you decide to be busy. So, I tracked you down here. Not an easy feat, I'll have you know."

Tory grinned back. "I've just been working, that's it."

"And avoiding all people. I don't want that, you know. You need to be social; you're a social person. I don't like that us separating has caused you to withdraw into yourself."

With a sigh, Tory leaned back. "It isn't that. I just need a few days to calibrate. I'm not used to all these emotions. I haven't dated a lot, but usually when the break-up happens ... I dunno, it's cleaner? Easier? This hasn't been easy."

Mildred's face hardened as her mouth pushed together into a firm line. After a moment she sighed. "It's been hard on me as well. At one point, I decided witches were real as well as wolves and that you'd placed a spell on me."

After a quick double check to make sure their corner was still just the two of them, Tory bit her bottom lip, then said, "Witches are real. But I'm not one. And I don't *think* I put a spell on you, but I'm not entirely sure."

Mildred's jaw dropped. "Can you start over, unwrap that, and try again?"

Tory laughed. "Gods above, I haven't laughed in days. Witches are real. There are white and black witches. We think the concoction is created by the black witches. Part of the recipe is a spell, so there'll be no recreating it even if we can get it nipped in the bud."

"You're not kidding, are you?"

"Nope." A lightness filled Tory at their familiar banter, and she smiled.

"Are there vampires and, I don't know, phoenixes?" Mildred's hands flew out to the side, questioningly.

"Phoenixes? That's where your mind goes?"

"What, they're amazing, rising from the ashes. Wouldn't it be majestic?"

Tory slumped. "No to the walking dead. Everyone wants vampires, but no, once someone dies, they stay dead. No zombies either." She sipped her water. "Just witches and wolves."

"I guess that's enough. But phoenixes would've been cool."

A grumble bubbled up from Tory's gut and she shook her head. "Whatever."

Mildred threw her head back and laughed. "Okay, fair enough. So, were you bitten? Is that how you became a werewolf?"

"No, I was born this way. A lot of us were. There are bitten wolves as well, but mostly it's hereditary."

"So, if you were born this way, then your parents know. But with the bitten wolves, can they tell anyone? Friends, family? Anyone? Or are they forced into the life of lies and deceit?" Her lip twitched up in a sneer at the final words.

Tory flinched at the harsh word. She'd felt like things had been getting better during their conversation, but obviously Mildred was still upset. "Look, I'm sorry I kept this part of my life from you. It's one of the first pack laws. I know I hurt you, and I wish I could change things, but I can't."

"Would you do things differently?"

"I don't know. I'm not going to lie to you. I know you think I lie, but I don't. Wolves can smell lies, and it makes us much more honest in our dealings. Telling people our secret is a process."

Mildred looked down at her hands. "Would you ever have told me?"

Tory froze, her wolf howling inside her. Her body started to tremble. "I want to say yes, but the answer really would've depended on you."

Dark eyes met hers. "What does that mean?"

She bit her lip. "It means. Gods, this is hard." She slipped her hands across the table and captured

Mildred's. "Over the past few weeks, you've captured my heart. You stole the heart of my wolf. We're all in, Mildred. I'm in love with you. I know it's too soon and I sound crazy, but with wolves it happens fast. And—"

Mildred cut her off with a kiss, slow and deep. She returned the kiss, wrapping her arms around Mildred's neck, and it felt like she was coming home.

Chapter 38 - Joining the Pack
Mildred

The following weekend, Mildred met with Tamsin at the pack house. She was tired of being hurt, angry and scared. She realized Tory had won her heart, too. She wanted to fight for the sassy blue-haired woman, and the only way to do that was to understand her better.

"You want to join the werewolf classes?" Tamsin asked, handing her a mug of some of the best coffee she'd ever had. *Damn, Tory was right!*

They sat in the kitchen. Besides her and Tamsin, Tory and another woman, Georgette, joined them. Someone had made hashbrowns and eggs with a side of roasted peppers. The food was as delicious as the coffee.

Mildred gazed at everyone sitting around the table and shrugged. "I think so. I'd like to better understand what all this means. Being separated from Tory hurt my heart. We haven't known each other long enough for that, right? But it did. So, if we're going to be together, I'd like to understand all of this."

Georgette laughed. "The classes are the best way. And watching the superpowers will either scare you off or make you one of us."

Tory rolled her eyes and shook her head. "Ignore her."

Tamsin smirked at them. "Okay, I think this will work. Lessons are at six every morning. You'll be with Cyrus, which will be fun all on its own. One of us will lead. Now that that's settled, was there anything else?"

"One more thing." Tory stood to refill her coffee before sitting back down. "I don't know if you spoke with Bexlee, but I think I've figured out how we can identify black witches."

An eyebrow flew up to Tamsin's hairline, and she tilted her head. "Is that so? They've been elusive—losing the herbal, earthy witch scent when their magic turns to death and decay."

"Yeah, well, I've been working with Nia for all those months, and she always smelled like old, dead leather."

Georgette leaned back, narrowing her eyes and crossing her arms over her chest. "Huh, that's a kind of death, isn't it? That's really interesting. How did you figure it out?"

"Well, she wore old boots, so I thought that was the smell, until one day she wasn't wearing the boots and still had the smell ... oh, and she tried to kill me with poisoned water."

"Oh, it's that last bit that gave it away, isn't it?" Georgette laughed.

"Yeah, pretty much."

After two weeks of learning about werewolves, Mildred decided: she was all in. She understood why the other woman kept her secret and why not letting the information out casually was important.

She'd also learned why their split had hurt them so much. Paige, Tamsin's partner, had sat her down and laid out her theory about wolves and their partners. Once a wolf finds the one they want to spend the rest of their life with, that's it, they were done looking. It had to do with the wolf magic. Not only that, but that connection went both ways if the partner agreed, regardless of whether they were wolf or not. The bond was strong and, as they learned, fighting it was almost impossible.

Also, during the two weeks, Cyrus decided to join the pack. He didn't want to become a lone wolf. Despite the restriction of being part of the pack, he preferred to enjoy the benefits of the werewolf community.

Then Mildred asked to have a meeting with Tamsin and Tory.

Tamsin sat with her in the backyard. Pack house was full, and finding privacy was difficult. "What do you need?"

Mildred shrank back, intimidated by the alpha of the Pacific Pack. She was strength and beauty. *So are you. That's how your mother raised you.*

She licked her lips. "I would like to join your pack. As a wolf."

"You know, this isn't a decision you can unmake," Tamsin warned.

"I want to be Tory's mate, to the fullest extent possible. I know what I'm asking. It's what I want."

A smile spread across her face. "Alright then, welcome to the pack."

Find the Next Book
Mystical Science, here

https://mybook.to/MysticalScience

Where to Find Harlowe Frost
Thanks for reading!
Find more of my books on my website:
http://hannahwillowauthor.com

You can also find me on:
Twitter: @hannahwillow217
Instagram: @hannahwillow217
Facebook Hannah Willow

About the Author

Harlowe Frost has been a teacher at both the high school and college level. Her parents instilled a love of reading from a young age. She grew up in the queer community. Her favorite genre growing up was fantasy and science fiction, that is, until she discovered urban fantasy and paranormal romance. What she never found in those books was the diversity in background, gender identity, and sexuality she saw in the people around her. She decided if she couldn't find that in what she read, then she would write it herself. This started her writing paranormal romance with a LGBTQ+ background

www.ingramcontent.com/pod-product-compliance
Lightning Source LLC
Chambersburg PA
CBHW061615190726
48288CB00007B/2327